# THE ROD OF LIGHT

A SCIENCE FICTION NOVEL BY
## BARRINGTON J. BAYLEY

ARBOR HOUSE
NEW YORK

For Elise Pechersky
who prompted me to finish

First published by Arbor House in 1987

Copyright © 1985 by Barrington J. Bayley

Manufactured in the United States of America

Library of Congress Cataloging in Publication Data

Bayley, Barrington J.
    The rod of light/by Barrington J. Bayley.
      p.   cm.
    ISBN: 0-87795-935-8
    I. Title.
PR6052.A875R6   1987        87-27236
823′.914—dc19               CIP

10 9 8 7 6 5 4 3 2 1

1 Reddened and magnified, the sun had descended through a clear sky and was poised over the edge of the hilly landscape, when its radiance picked out a burnished metal figure that had climbed to the summit of a turfed ridge. The traveller paused, and for a considerable while gazed intently at the mellowed orb, as though endeavouring to return its eternal stare. For his eyes, like the evening sun itself, were also red and glowing, and seemed to project the same intense presence.

His body was bronze-black, man-shaped and handsome, decorated from head to foot with scroll-like engravings. The face was an enigma: an immobile machine-visage, its expression stern yet hinting at tenderness. Suddenly the robot's head tilted up, as his attention was caught by a glint of golden light. The sun had caught the underside of a plane's wing, moving slowly on the end of a newly appeared contrail.

Jasperodus stepped back into the shadow of the ridge, and waited half-kneeling, one arm rested on a bended knee, hoping that the plane's pilot had not, in turn, spotted him.

When he emerged the plane was gone, and for the first time he looked down the west-facing slope.

He saw a compact, cirque-like valley. Toward the bottom of the slope, a little to his left, stood a building, the first he had come across in this wilderness. It was about the size of a three-storey villa but had the form of a ziggurat, constructed of well-fitting stone blocks, with a porch projecting from one side. In front of this porch stood an oddly shaped cowl, also carved from stone, which acted as a windshield for an elegant bowl mounted on a pedestal. In the bowl, a pale flame burned.

The place had the appearance of a temple. Jasperodus

was surprised to find an intact and apparently inhabited building of any kind in so isolated a spot. He estimated its age at no more than a hundred years, in which case it was of no interest to him archaeologically, having been built long after the collapse of the Old Empire. He would have passed it by, had not his sighting of the aircraft disconcerted him. These bare hillsides offered little concealment from what could possibly be a photographic reconnaissance with robots as its object. He would try to take shelter in the building until dark.

Making his way down the slope, he reached the porch, lingering to inspect the fire in the bowl. The wick was a fleecy wad floating in perfumed oil. The flame burned steadily. It was alive with sparkling flecks which swarmed up it to vanish at its fringe, releasing a powerful scent of roses.

Jasperodus found the arrangement charming. Cautiously he stepped into the porch, to find the passage blocked by a slab of reddish stone he recognised as porphyry. He pounded on it with his fist, tuning up his hearing so as to detect any response. He heard nothing, and began to think the building unoccupied after all, but then there came the hiss of a penumatic mechanism, and the slab drew aside.

In its place was revealed a silvery panel, or screen, on which an image was slowly forming. It was of a tall, slender man in a light blue gown. He would be aged about sixty, with flaxen hair falling to his shoulders. His eyes matched the gown: pale blue. They were hypnotically steady as they rested on Jasperodus, and his lips moved.

'What brings a servant of Ahriman to the Temple of Light?' asked a resonant, though rather high-pitched voice.

Jasperodus took a moment before replying. 'I am no one's servant,' he said evenly. 'I am a free construct. May I shelter under your roof for a while?'

The gowned man looked him up and down thoughtfully,

though no camera to convey his image was visible. 'You ask for shelter? Do you feel the cold, robot?'

'No, I do not feel the cold,' Jasperodus said. Suddenly impatient, he reached out and clawed down the silvery screen. It was silky and ripped easily. But ten feet further along, the passageway was again blocked by a second slab of porphyry.

'It is understandable that you should fear me,' he said, disgruntled. 'Very well, then, I shall bother you no further.'

Soon it would be dark. He decided to remain in the porch till after sunset, and then be on his way. But now the man spoke again, his voice slightly slurred.

'I do not fear you, robot. Come, enter the Temple of Light. After all, you are a creature.'

With a hiss the second block of porphyry slid aside. Jasperodus went forward. Behind him, the barrier closed up again.

He found himself in a simply furnished room, the walls and ceiling painted sky-blue. The man whose image had appeared on the screen stood beside a low table, laid with a half-full wine decanter and a glass goblet.

Clearly this was a living chamber. An ottoman, long enough to double as a sleeping couch, stood against one wall. Domestic articles — silver cups and platters, bottles, wooden caskets, combs and brushes — occupied a shelf running the length of the wall opposite. Otherwise the furniture consisted only of the table and two stout timber chairs.

There were no windows — the ziggurat did not appear to possess any. Lighting was by means of a bright oil lamp hanging from the ceiling, close to a flue for carrying away the fumes, while ventilation grills were set high in the walls.

The blue-eyed man was regarding Jasperodus with a peculiarly intense expression. He reached out, refilling the goblet from the decanter. Then he sat down, gesturing.

'Be seated, Ahriman.'

Though equally comfortable standing, Jasperodus gingerly settled his weight in the remaining chair. It cracked, but held.

'My name is not Ahriman.'

'All robots should be called Ahriman,' said the temple-keeper, for this was what Jasperodus by now presumed him to be. He was, it was becoming evident, somewhat drunk. 'But never mind. What is your business in this region?'

'I am an archaeologist,' Jasperodus told him, 'on my way to join my assistants who are carrying out a dig to the north-west of here. I travel on foot to be less conspicuous. As you may know, the Borgor Alliance has been making incursions into this area, and Borgors destroy robots out of hand.'

The templar nodded. 'So I believe. You are an archaeologist, you say? But also you claim to be a free construct. What interest could archaeology possibly have for you?'

'I study the past to seek the cause of historical change,' the robot said in an intentionally neutral voice. 'We emerge from a turbulent dark age. Why did the splendid Rule of Tergov that preceded it collapse like a house of cards? Is there a law of history that brings calamity just when civilisation seems about to fulfil itself? This is what I aim to find out.'

'I repeat, why should you?' The templar sounded querulous, and Jasperodus became uneasy. Had his wish to learn something of the temple made him divulge his own circumstances too freely?

'I owe it to those who made me,' he said simply.

'You have an instruction? So you are not so free after all.'

'There is no instruction. It is of my own choosing.'

The man grunted. He almost scowled. 'Then this is an unusual sentiment. What can the advance of human civilisation mean to you? You are a robot. Not a man.'

'And the difference . . . ?'

8

Making a dismissive face, the templar gulped wine, spilling it from the corners of his mouth and dribbling it down his gown. Then, with an air of self-possession, he brushed away the drop.

'Can you tell me something about this place?' Jasperodus asked. 'The Temple of Light, you called it. Also you insisted on forcing an identification with someone called "Ahriman" upon me. This is the mythic projection, perhaps? Is Ahriman one of the robotic gods?'

'It could be said that in a sense he is,' the templar agreed, apparently struck by the thought. 'By your very nature you cannot help but serve him. Even if you imagine you serve the light, you cannot help but serve the darkness.'

Having drained the wine cup, the templar put it down but this time did not refill it. 'Do you seek ancient knowledge, robot? Then you have come to the right place, because this is the last temple of the world's first and only true religion — the religion of Zoroaster, founded on an objective knowledge of the real nature of the world.'

'I would not have attributed "objective knowledge" to any religion,' Jasperodus said pensively.

'You would be correct as to the others. They are all corruptions or misunderstandings of some aspect of Zoroastrian teaching.'

'What, exactly, is the purpose of this temple?' Jasperodus enquired. 'Is it a place of instruction? Do you have pupils?'

The other smiled, his parchment-like skin creasing. 'I was a pupil once. There are no more, except the occasional wayfarer. Come, let me show you my one and only function.'

The man rose, and beckoned. Deeper into the temple they went, to where the light was dim and the passages were of bare stone. Then the templar drew aside a curtain and ushered the hulking robot into the inner sanctum.

They were in a dome-shaped chamber, the concave ceiling painted midnight-blue and pricked with bright points of light to represent stars. The centre of the chamber was occupied by a fan-shaped flame which burned with a hissing sound and threw off an almost overpowering scent, again of roses. Like a peacock's tail blazed this fan, reaching almost to half the height of the chamber. Yet for all its size its glow was soft. It failed to dispel the dimness of the room.

The flame too contained brighter flecks, like those in the flame of the shrine outside the temple but larger. They soared, danced and gyrated, and vanished as they reached the fire's fringe.

'Does the flame inspire you, robot?' came the templar's dry voice. 'It should. It is the symbol of what your kind gropes for and covets. The fire is the fire of consciousness that roars through the universe and brings awareness to transient forms Those sparks you see are individual souls, born of the fire and glowing briefly, only to vanish forever when their course is done. You asked me what is the difference between man and robot. You know very well, I think.'

Jasperodus felt chill at these words. He turned to confront his host. The man stared back at him, eyes of pale blue directly meeting the red eyes of the robot.

'How *would* I know?' Jasperodus demanded.

The templar made no answer but turned and strolled from the chamber.

Back in the living room he took his place as before and resumed drinking heavily. Jasperodus began to get the impression that he drank constantly.

'Well, now you know my function. I am the last keeper of the sacred flame, the last worshipper of Ahura Mazda. With my death, the light of the world is symbolically quenched.'

'You live here alone?' asked Jasperodus.

'I know of no neighbour within a hundred miles.'

'How do you provide for yourself?'

'Ancient science.' The templar smiled. 'There is a

garden on the other side of the hill, covered with a glass dome. It contains special tanks and trays for growing food quickly and easily. There I also ferment my wine.'

'I am interested in this teaching of Zoroaster. Tell me something about it.'

'Indeed, I know you are,' the templar said, with what Jasperodus thought annoying mysteriousness. He prevaricated, but when Jasperodus pressed him further he proved more than willing to expatiate.

The world he said, consisted of a cosmic struggle between two opposed and roughly equal powers, personified by the gods Ahura Mazda, prince of light, and Ahriman, prince of darkness. By light was meant the realm of consciousness or spirit. By darkness was meant the realm of unconsciousness, of dense materiality and blind mechanical forces. From the beginning of time the war between the two had gone on without pause, as each sought to subdue the other and make itself ruler of all existence.

Though the conflict took many forms, the surfaces of planets were a front-line of special interest. Here the two principles struggled in a kind of scrum, mixing and mingling. From the unharmonious mixture there arose organic life, compounded of awareness and gross matter both.

When Jasperodus asked with what weapons the gods fought, the templar seemed amused. 'The angels of Ahura Mazda do not confont the dark directly,' he said. 'Insofar as we are concerned, it is through the affairs and hearts of men that they contend with the dark angels of Ahriman. What are the two currents in the human psyche? There is the striving towards the light, that is, for greater consciousness. And there is also submission to the powers of unconsciousness, that is, animal ignorance, coarse cruelty, tyranny, failure to perceive. The struggle between the two is the struggle between Ahura Mazda and Ahriman. And it is there, in the affairs of men, that Ahriman will shortly have his victory.'

'So you are pessimistic about the future of mankind?'

'I speak with sure knowledge that we enter the final phase of the struggle here on Earth. You see, the cosmic war is capable of subtle involvements. The aim of pure consciousness is eventually the rule and command matter in all its aspects. What else is the purpose of science? Likewise, the aim of the material principle is to imprison and enslave consciousness. In this the adversary has shown cunning beyond compare. He takes religion, originally a system for kindling new consciousness, and makes of it a system for totally imprisoning human awareness. Now he has a new weapon with which he can outflank, invade and conquer the realm of Ahura Mazda, a weapon that nothing can stop. You know what I speak of, do you not, when I describe this weapon?'

'No, I do not,' Jasperodus said.

'I speak of yourself. I speak of the robot. A complete simulacrum of a man! Able to do anything a man can do, to think and even to feel! But lacking consciousness. The perfect Ahrimanic creature! Intelligent, but without any spark of the sacred flame! Robots are Ahriman's new servants, and in their millions they will comprise his armies. Mimicking the light, Ahriman will overcome the light.'

In reply, Jasperodus chose his words carefully. 'It is true that there are now large numbers of free constructs, and that these have begun to design and make a new generation of constructs less tractable to human orders than the old,' he said. 'But as for the emergence of a world-system of self-directed constructs to challenge mankind, I do not think this could happen. As you point out, robots are not conscious. When men and robots meet, it is still the robots who become the subordinates before very long.'

'*You* do not give me any impression of compliance whatsoever,' the templar murmured. 'In any case, the matter does not end there. Did I not say that the darkness seeks to capture the light? The robot hungers for

12

consciousness. And so he moves against the light, to seize the light. Thus will Ahura Mazda be clapped in a steel dungeon, a prisoner of metal, and Ahriman his jailer.'

Jasperodus shook his head. 'You are quite wrong. Robots do not have any conception of consciousness. For them it is a meaningless word.'

'*Ordinary* robots do not,' the templar said quietly. 'But there are robots of extreme mental subtlety, and some of them know what is lacking in them. After all, a construct's level of intelligence is now only a technical issue. There are robots far exceeding the mental capacity possible for a human being.'

A sense of amazement was coming over Jasperodus as he grasped what the man was saying, but again he shook his head. 'You apparently believe artificial consciousness to be the next step in construct development. I can tell you categorically that artificial consciousness is a scientific impossibility. It has been proved so.'

'Well, I am no robotician,' said the templar dreamily, 'but I have met better minds than mine who believe this "impossibility" could be circumvented. *Ahrimanic minds.*' With a sudden, almost aggressive movement the man noisily drained his goblet and banged it down on the table beside him. '*What of you, for instance?*' he demanded loudly. 'We sit here talking of consciousness, and *you* seem to have no difficulty over the meaning of the word. One might almost think *you* were conscious. At any rate, it tells me something about you. It tells me that your tale of archaeological work is only a cover. You go to join Gargan, perhaps.'

'Gargan?' Jasperodus queried.

'A construct, like yourself.' The templar's eyes began to unfocus and his eyelids to drop. 'He, too, asked for instruction in the doctrine of Zoroaster. Only he did not pretend to come upon me by accident.'

Jasperodus fell silent. Disconcerting as the templar's

statements were, he was beginning to lose the drift of his meanderings.

'Looking on robots as you do,' he remarked, 'why did you allow me into Ahura Mazda's temple?'

'Why not? Ahriman will enter the inner sanctum. Ahriman will seize the sacred flame. For thousands of years the great knowledge has been preserved in secret sects and brotherhoods. Now I am alone — yes, I am the last of the mages; and when I am gone there will be no one to keep the sacred flame. I bear you no malice, robot. You are a creature, and though you are born of the machinations of Ahriman, you cannot help that. The two gods are equal in stature.'

'You speak, of course, of Ahriman's victory on the planet Earth,' Jasperodus said. 'What of the outcome on a cosmic scale?'

'Ultimate victory for either side is a distant prospect,' the mage murmured. 'It would change the character of nature, bringing the universal drama to an end . . . '

He swayed in his chair and his head drooped. Throughout his explanations, the blue-gowned Zoroastrian had shown a remarkable ability to seem incoherently drunk one minute and incisively sober the next. Perhaps he had some method of metabolising alcoholic poisons out of his system with unusual rapidity, Jasperodus thought.

But now he seemed spent, and laid his head on the table with a loud sigh, cradling it in his arms. This failed to bring him to rest, however, and his body slid slowly and majestically floorward.

Jasperodus rose, gathered him up and placed the sleeping form on the ottoman. He stood there, reflecting.

The flame. He felt an urge to see the flame again.

Hurriedly he went back down the stone passage to come again to the inner sanctum, and stared spellbound into the luminous fire. The flame's fan shape, he observed, was due to a slit-like metal burner which emitted the combustible oil in the form of a vapour or spray — the device was more elaborate than the lamp outside the porch. And the symbolism was exquisite! The flame hissed, it roared, it wavered, but it never lost shape. Jasperodus traced the course of a spark as it caught fire an inch from the orifice, a glowing star that danced and soared, soon to be extinguished in the outer darkness.

The Zoroastrian creed, too, was fascinating. Jasperodus was much taken by its description of existence as universal war, a war that was as hazardous as it was unceasing. It differed radically from other mystic doctrines he was familiar with, which generally depicted nature as issuing from some all-embracing principle of unity or harmony — a view, he now recognised, which contradicted the facts, and clothed a core of delusive sentimentality.

Slowly, head bent in thought, he returned to the living chamber. Looking down on the sleeping templar, he debated within himself what he should do.

It had startled him to hear the mage practically — or so it seemed to him — accuse him of being conscious. If so, this aspect of their conversation was much more extraordinary than the Zoroastrian doctrine itself. One would have to believe that the temple keeper could sense another conscious mind directly through the legendary faculty of telepathy, much as some robots were able to commune by brain-to-brain radio.

It was true what Jasperodus had said: consciousness could not be artificially generated. It was immaterial and therefore uncreatable. But on one other point he had, by implication, lied. He himself was what he had denied was possible: a conscious robot.

There was a great secret, of which he was guardian: true, consciousness could not be made; but it was malleable. It could be treated, melted down, ducted into a special retort, transferred from one vessel to another. In that process lay the source of Jasperodus' being.

Two had been involved in it: the genius who had discovered the principle, and his childless wife. Sad at their

15

childlessness, they had found a new way to satisfy the urge to leave progeny. First, they had constructed Jasperodus' powerful brain and body. then had come the arcane infusion: each, man and woman, donating half a soul to mix a new, original soul in the metal body; and thereby becoming Jasperodus' father and mother.

They, too, had used the analogy of fire to describe consciousness, calling it supernal fire, cosmic fire. They were dead now, and with them had died all knowledge of how to work the psychic alchemy. Jasperodus, their son and sole confidant, was sworn — whatever it might cost him in personal loneliness — never to disclose that such a thing was even possible. His father had judged such knowledge too dangerous to mankind.

If he were to suspect now that the templar had divined his secret . . .

Jasperodus raised his fist. One blow would silence the sleeping man forever.

No, the idea was not plausible. The mage could not have guessed the truth. It was simply that he had fallen into a trap common among those who attached themselves to doctrines: he saw verification of his beliefs in everything that happened. Convinced that robots were on the verge of acquiring consciousness, he imagined it in every robot he met. More than likely he was half-crazed, an embittered hermit faced with the dying-out of his sect.

Jasperodus let fall his hand. By now night would have fallen, and there was nothing to detain him further. Searching the living room he found, behind a wall hanging, a set of levers for operating the porphyry doors. He cleared the corridor and walked through to the open air, where he climbed the wall of the cirque in near-darkness.

A three-quarters moon rode in the sky. The wan wash it cast on the landscape was the ghost of light rather than light itself. The indistinct hills and vales showed dim and silvery, seeming unreal, preternaturally silent, as if they were not seen at all.

The mage had given him a Zoroastrian aphorism: 'The sun rules the light, the moon rules the dark.' The dark, if Jasperodus had understood him correctly, was the realm of the robotic mind. Was this glimmering moonlit landscape, then, symbolic of the robot's world? Seen but not really seen? He had often tried to imagine what genuine construct existence was like. Logically it was not like anything — it was not there at all. Yet it did contain thought; there was deliberation in it, and a machine awareness that was like a passive reflection of human consciousness, just as moonlight was a passive reflection of sunlight. In the same way the moon created a spurious version of the daylit world, so perhaps there was a reflected fictitious world of construct perception, and if one could look into this world perhaps one would see, as it were, a realm under the moon, not quite visible, mysteriously passive and asleep. Except that on this landscape, the sun never rose. Were it not that they knew no other world, one could pity robots for their cold, unillumined non-existence.

A cloud drew across the moon and blotted out the ghost landscape. Tuning up his vision to accommodate his eyes to the lower light level, Jasperodus trudged on.

Three days saw him out of the range of hills and onto a fairly level plain. Shortly after dawn of the next day, he approached the site of the archaeological dig.

It consisted chiefly of a long trench into which broad steps had been cut. Constructs moved slowly and carefully in the excavation, looking from a distance like metallic grubs. On the far side rested a large earthmover, and beyond that an air transporter that had brought the team here.

Jasperodus noticed that several craters, seemingly from bomb blasts, dotted the area. He sought out the team leader, a gangling figure by the name of Glyco.

'Well?' he demanded without preamble.

'We shall be unable to remain much longer,' Glyco

informed him in a silvery voice. 'Yesterday we were attacked by Borgor planes, in spite of our attempting to camouflage the site with a ground sheet. Our missiles drove them off, but they are bound to be back.'

Jasperodus was rueful. His journey had been wasted. 'Best make preparations to depart. Are there any noteworthy finds?'

Glyco led him to a large awning. Beneath it numerous objects and fragments were laid out. 'It is hard to say just what this installation once was,' he said. 'Not a town, not a single dwelling, not a factory. It seems somehow a mixture of all three. We have turned up many artifacts made of this curious substance.'

He handed Jasperodus an empty casing that was surprisingly light — lighter by far than any metal or wood, except perhaps balsa. Its pale lavender surface was perfectly smooth and shiny.

Jasperodus nodded. 'Then material was used extensively both before and during the Rule of Tergov. It is a hydrocarbon. In the course of manufacture it can be made plastic but quickly hardens, so it could very easily be moulded or pressed.'

'One more example of Tergov's technical elegance, then? Still, I had hoped I was showing you something new.'

'I am afraid not.' Jasperodus flexed the casing, admiring its strength-to-weight ratio. The material, known generically as 'plastic', was derived from a mineral oil once found in widespread natural deposits. Exhaustion of the natural oil reserves had forced manufacturers to revert to the more awkwardly worked metal and wood. Otherwise Jasperodus himself would probably have consisted of this 'plastic', as would nearly all robots – for such had been the case a thousand or more years ago.

For once there was something to be said for the cruder technology of recent times. Jasperodus liked his body of weighty steel.

18

Glyco handed him another object. 'Is this more informative?'

It was a thin sheet of gold, measuring about one foot by two. Etched on it was what appeared to be a short extract from an oscillograph recording, marked by regular vertical lines that presumably represented time periods. Waves of various frequencies marched across the sheet, superimposed so that troughs and peaks met and diverged at random. Under the graph was a text inscribed in logic symbols, the neat signs of which also littered the graph itself.

Jasperodus examined the sheet closely. He had sent his team here because old maps had led him to think it might be the site of an ancient academic institute for the study of social change. Tergov had not fallen altogether unresistingly; learned men had suspected that collapse might be imminent, and had tried to gather data that might be used to allay the catastrophe.

'It is a graph of social periodicities,' he announced. 'Impossible to interpret, unfortunately, since the parameters are missing. I cannot even say if the variations are economic or psychological . . . do you have more of these sheets?'

'Not so far, Jasperodus.'

'Well, keep looking.' He studied the graph again. Interesting that it should have been thought worth inscribing on gold . . . The ancients had set great store on the idea of periodic cycles, applying them to all kinds of phenomena, including history. There had even been an attempt to ascribe social variations to changes in solar activity, by matching the rise and fall of trade levels to sunspot cycles. Superficially there was some merit in the idea: sunspots, like societies, were apt to display regular periodicity for centuries at a time, only to break rhythm suddenly and produce violent flurries, or else disappear altogether for a while. There was no evidence of unusual solar activity to coincide with the onset of the Dark Age, however.

Jasperodus set down the plate as another of the robots

19

entered, speaking in a voice of subdued agitation. 'Aircraft approach from the north! We have counted fifteen blips!'

Questioningly Glyco turned his head to Jasperodus. 'This would seem to be a more determined attack than previously.'

'Quite plainly we will not be left in peace to pursue our researches,' Jasperodus decided. 'Give the order to depart. Get everything you can aboard the transporter.'

He stepped from beneath the awning. Some distance beyond the trench two robots were manning the radar set and missile board. Almost immediately there was a WHOOSH and a slim rocket shot from its rack, gathering speed to disappear over the horizon, closely followed by a second.

The small but efficient defence unit would delay the attackers for the extra few minutes needed to make a getaway. Glyco bawled commands, striding hither and thither. Constructs crawled hastily up out of the trench. The huge earthmover, self-directed but of low mentality, caught the sense of urgency and auto-started, trundling to and fro in panic.

While the hoard of artifacts and photographs were being piled aboard the air carrier Glyco returned to Jasperodus. 'There will be no time to dismantle the earthmover. It will have to be abandoned.'

'It cannot be helped.'

Loosing off their remaining target-seeking missiles, the defence robots ran for the transporter, which had already ignited its engines. At that moment a Borgor plane came spearing over the horizon: a grey, thruster-driven arrowhead. The last missile released swerved to engage it, and for a while the two performed an aerial dance until the more nimble rocket struck home, knocking the injured attack plane to the ground.

Behind it, streaking close to the landscape, came a second plane, this time to be greeted from the carrier by a fast-firing cannon which zipped out a line of tracers.

Shortly another carrier-mounted weapon came into action: a beam gun whose dimly glowing ray wavered about the sky.

Neither succeeded in hitting the plane, but it banked and sped away like a startled bird. Borgor pilots would disdain to risk their lives simply to destroy robots. Just the same, Jasperodus told himself that his long journey to the archaeological site had all been for nothing. Perhaps he should have travelled by air after all . . . But no, that would only have brought the Borgors down on the team even sooner.

In the moments before the transporter lifted away from the dirt, he swung aboard. The carrier little resembled a conventional aircraft such as would be used to convey humans, but looked more like a winged girder bridge with swivel-mounted engines distributed one at either end and one in the middle. There were no cabins, only a cargo box; windshields welded to the girder-work provided the only protection for the passengers. Behind these, robots clung to girders as the vehicle moved forwards and began to gather speed.

Jasperodus glanced below. The earthmover had tried to join the general rush to board the carrier. It seemed desperate not to be left behind; as the carrier soared away it continued to charge haplessly after it, treads gouging twin tracks across the plain.

**2** Crossing the rolling hills, the air transporter flew for some hours over a semi-arid region. Eventually it neared a prominent rubbly hill that protruded out of the middle of a flat plain.

A curious feature of the hill was the natural earth ringwall that surrounded it, looking like nothing so much as the wall of a lunar crater. Outside this rampart there sprawled for miles in every direction a sheet metal shanty town, rambling and disordered. The carrier slanted down over sheds and shacks, the scream of its barrel-shaped thrusters falling to a purling moan as it alighted on a stretch of wasteground, the jar of its landing dislodging numbers of robots from their perches and tumbling them to the cindery surface. They staggered to their feet flexing their limbs, whose lubrication had been made stiff by the coldness of the journey.

Jasperodus, on the other hand, dropped lithely from the girderwork and approached the disembarking Glyco.

'Unload all the findings and store them,' he ordered. 'I will examine them later.' Glyco nodded, his blue-sheened skull glinting in the sunlight.

Jasperodus strode off towards his private dwelling about two miles away, entering what to a human would have looked like a disorganised slum. To some extent the ramshackle appearance of the shanty city was misleading: robots did not invest their energy in architecture. For them, buildings were an afterthought, erected as a precaution against rust or rain, to prevent their possessions from being blown away, or merely in imitation of their one-time human masters. Otherwise, a bare encampment might have served as well.

The first district Jasperodus had to traverse was the quarter of the indolents. Robots had the same tendency as

22

humans to congregate like with like. Lounging in the doorways of dull sheds of zinc and iron were constructs marked by an habitual lassitude, a few of whom offered languid greeting as a traveller went by. They felt no boredom, and would remain inactive for months at a time unless nudged into motion by some outside stimulus.

Their passivity was not, however, typical of robotkind. More telling was the industriousness visible on the central hill that loomed through the dust and heat haze, its rough surface running with glowing rivulets of metal that were being smelted directly out of the mass and guided to foundries and workshops inside the ringwall.

The hill, a huge lump of iron, nickel and other metals in lesser amounts, including rare earths, was the source of all the building material in the robot city, and had also supplied the bodies of many of its inhabitants. It was, in fact, an impacted asteroid shard, one of hundreds scattered about the world. Jasperodus had pieced together the story of their arrival on Earth, and they were testimony to the most risk-ridden period in all history.

The bombardment dated from the last days of the Rule of Tergov. Earth's minerals were long since exhausted: for centuries she had imported all her raw materials from elsewhere in the solar system. Evidently there had been someone in those last desperate days – someone who still commanded resources and had the power to act – who knew that organised society was irretrievably lost and that the Dark Period, as it became known, lay ahead. That same someone had also realized that, without metals, Earth could never again give rise to a technological culture.

The solution was a ruthless programme to reprovision the planet before it was too late. A number of ferrous asteroids had been deflected from their transmartian orbits and placed in near-Earth orbit, where they were broken into smaller pieces and directed into the atmosphere.

The horrific side-effects of an act of this kind were

almost beyond imagining. Although the terminal velocities of the asteroid chunks were low by astronomical standards – or else they would have devastated the whole Earth – the loss of life must have been appalling (even if only adding to the slaughter produced by civil strife). About half the shards had been aimed into sparsely inhabited regions; but the rest had been placed close to the predicted sites of future emergent cultures – close to river valleys, natural harbours, salt deposits and so on – which by the same token were already densely populated. Neither had the targeting, which it could be presumed tried to minimise damage wherever possible, always been accurate. In one case an asteroid had fallen squarely on a major city.

Who had decided upon the scheme? Who had implemented it? Civil authority had by then vanished. What technical resources remained were mostly in the hands of the warring factions, who would scarcely have interested themselves in long-term considerations ... Jasperodus' theory was that robots had been responsible for the project. No human would have had the nerve for it – it was too horrendous. A human would have hesitated, delayed, hoped for another solution ... until finally there was no longer the capability for taking action.

It must have been robots. Robots, servants of Tergov with an unbending sense of duty, had decided upon the necessity for the scheme, had planned it, had contrived to commandeer the equipment needed for it, and had carried it out. Alone, they had saved mankind from a perpetual stone age.

Or had they? It was not possible to be sure. More skills than they had anticipated, perhaps, had survived the Dark Period – the art of robotics itself, for instance. And there was still scrap metal lying about in the wrecked cities of old Tergov, though mostly converted to rust. Perhaps this would have sustained mankind through to the early redevelopment of space travel, making the mineral resources of the solar system once more available.

Perhaps. Perhaps not. In either case a world poor in metals would have had few robots. As it was, the present upsurge in robotic activity was entirely due to the presence of the asteroid deposits. They were what enabled robots to manufacture robots with a fervour not too different from a reproductive urge. They provided the physical resource for a construct civilisation that was developing its own customs, its own obsessions, and which was destined to mutate considerably away from its human origins, if it was not destroyed first by the human nations around it.

Jasperodus left the indolents' quarter behind him. From all around him came the noises of the township's activity – noises of metal, a susurration of clinking, clanking and clanging, of banging and gonging, of dragging of sheet on sheet, mingled with an occasional shout, cry or bellow, the purr or thump of an engine. He walked through a market area where citizens bartered products made in their personal workshops: toys, scientific instruments, curiosities or wholly novel devices (robots, not needing to earn their livings beyond the occasional replacement isotope battery, had much time for projects of an experimental or desultory nature), small doll-robots which took the place of pets in construct society, paltry in intelligence but endowed with endearing mannerisms. Heavier industry was concentrated closer to the iron-nickel mountain. There were to be found spacious workshops belonging to organised companies of robots, and from which there would typically emerge huge machines based on abstruse philosophical concepts which, more often than not, proved fallacious in practice. It did not seem to matter to the originators of these follies how often their ideas failed; they never counted the cost, either in time or effort, of anything they undertook. Wedged up against the ringwall that had been thrown up crater-fashion by the impact of the asteroid was also a ghetto district inhabited by non-androforms – wheeled, box-type, multi-ped, segmented and assorted robots, self-directed special-labour types scarcely classifiable as sentient (the earthmover abandoned at the archaeological site was one such) and a number of immobiles. Androforms largely disdained this social minority, for robot-makers, like nature, had discovered the humanoid shape to be the most convenient and versatile, and it had come to be associated with normality. The ghetto dwellers bore no grudge over their inferior status. They had no species feeling, and did not reproduce.

Jasperodus' route, however, took him not towards the ringwall but through a quarter where the production of new citizens was concentrated. The singed smell of hot metal was in the air, the smell of smoke and tempering steam. From long slant-roofed sheds rose the chimneys for the furnaces and rolling mills where sheet metal was made and body parts stamped out. Scattered around them were the homes and assembly shops of the robot-makers themselves, as well as the studies of those who specialised in design.

There was considerable reverence for those who spent their time creating their own kind. A crowd had gathered in a beaten-earth plaza, forcing Jasperodus to slow his pace. Suddenly it parted respectfully to make way for a figure which had stepped from a nearby assembly shed.

Though vaguely androform, it was a very specialised class of robot. It was, in fact, one of the new designer class, made especially for procreation. From huge shoulders extended clusters of long slender limbs bearing point-like tools for manipulating microcircuitry. There was no clearly defined head section, but the visual area was large. From it projected a variety of microscopes, photonic, electronic and acoustic, some more than two feet long, for peering into the minute world in which the designer worked (for every designer was also an assembler).

Its gait a ponderous lurch, the top-heavy construct walked carefully across the square and disappeared.

Jasperodus then saw why the crowd had gathered. A famed robot-maker by the name of Logos was hectoring it on his favourite theme: his belief in the eventual superiority of machines over organic beings. By way of demonstration he was pointing to a construct of his own manufacture who sat leaning against a pillar, one of the roof supports of Logos' dwelling.

The lolling robot was masturbating. Logos had provided it with a penis-like organ which it fondled with one hand, jogging its tubular sleeve up and down and plainly deriving a pleasurable sensation from the motion. The construct was probably low-grade. Unusually for a robot, it had eyelids: they drooped half-closed over dull orange eyes, quivering in self-absorbed ecstasy.

'See how the wretch spends his time!' thundered Logos. 'Instead of directing his activities into his environment, he turns them into a closed loop of self-gratification! He is both agent and patient of his world!

'This is a serious design flaw,' he continued in a quieter tone, 'which I deliberately incorporated in this unfortunate so as to demonstrate the root defect in human kind. For here we have the essence of human nature – it could not be otherwise, since the mainspring of any species lies in its method of reproduction. For humans, the act of procreation is one of sensory enjoyment, no more! The offspring are unintended byproducts! The parents lack the opportunity or even the wish to introduce improvements! And as the human is created, so he goes on. All his functions are tainted with self-titillation. His thought, too, is a form of masturbation! All attempts to break out of the circle are doomed, for in the long run humanity can only slide down the spiral of solipsism.

'But *we* are different.' The robot's voice became a thrumming murmur. '*Our* existence is the result of purposiveness and design. Each new generation can be an improvement on the old, and hence *our* thought need not be subject to a closed and feeble self-generating loop – it can go out, stamping itself upon the world, taking us further and further!' As he spoke Logos repeatedly flung his fist

27

away from his chest, as though throwing something out of himself. Many listening nodded, some clinking their forearms together in applause.

Near Jasperodus was a large tub filled with small domino-like squares of various colours. Thoughtfully he scooped up a handful and let them fall back in a rustling stream.

They were the basic building blocks of the robotic nervous system: microprocessors made of silicon, garnet and gallium arsenide, each chip, plate or wafer containing up to a hundred million logic units. In themselves they were comparatively easy to make, using special dies which could replicate them almost without limit. Similar dies, made during the Rule of Tergov, were what had enabled the art of robotics to last through the Dark Period, for even when technology fell to a low level logic chips had always been available as long as the dies remained in existence. But centuries had passed before it again became possible to manufacture new dies.

One sign of robots' increasing awareness of themselves as a distinct class of creature was the arising of robot religions. A plethora of robot gods had entered construct mentality, reflecting in specification the intellectual preoccupations of robots, but also some dim appreciation of the false position the construct occupied: a position intermediate between the world of dead, mechanical matter and the world of living beings. There was, for instance, Alumnabrax, a mythical being whose intellect was said to be perfect and able to solve equations of the infinite degree; whose body was made of an extraordinary celestial metal that could not even exist on Earth. Alumnabrax had never been manufactured, either by organic beings or by anyone else: he had manufactured himself by tampering with time. He lived among the stars, which he controlled by the excercise of his limitless technology.

Then there was Mekkan, who incongruously for a god

did not possess a mental function at all. Mekkan was purely and simply a production engine for churning out the stuff of worlds. Particles, atoms, quanta of radiant energy, whirlpools of gas, even complete suns and planets on occasion, all came pouring out of his delivery maw. All that existed had been manufactured in his busy innards, and without him nothing that was material had been made.

The worship of Mekkan might have appeared crude and ridiculous to human sensibilities, but actually it was a religious philosophy full of subtlety as understood by the robotic mind. Mekkan was the ultimate reality; the building blocks of matter he turned out in such copious quantities were sub-units of Mekkan himself, or at any rate identical copies of the same. All higher structures – worlds, systems, self-directed entities whether robotic or evolved organic – were in turn made up of those sub-units; were, in effect, merely rearrangements of the components of Mekkan, the great engine who saw nothing. Because of this, belief in Mekkan undercut the superiority of human beings by rendering their special quality superfluous and seeing everything as equally adventitious. In fact robots, rather than men, could be thought of as the natural children of the universe.

Religiosity was also beginning to surround the act of procreation. Already there was a designer god, incorporating all his tools in himself, and whose iconography was similar in appearance to the designer who had just passed with dignity through the crowd. And had not Logos named himself after yet another god, the god of pure information?

There was no doubt that religion was destined to play a large part in the developing robot culture, validating construct nature, giving mythic depth and ideation to a previously blank background. Proof could be found in the evangelising efforts of the various rival cults, whose methods, while highly successful, Jasperodus could not help but find amusing.

When living in human society he had been able to

observe the procedures of human missionaries. A favourite ploy of these had been to teach the prospective convert a certain prayer and persuade him to recite it, just as an experiment, or if he was a confirmed unbeliever as a favour, or indeed by means of any stratagem whatsoever. What was being relied on was the human mind's established susceptibility to self-suggestion. The prayers contained emotional charges, so expertly devised that there was nearly always some effect, and in a percentage of cases total belief followed in due course.

Robot evangelists parodied this practice fairly precisely. Typically they sought physically to readjust the brains of others so as to incorporate the approved beliefs in the form of cortical hardware; or to adminster data infusions to induce visions of the god or gnosis concerned, and so on. Some of the cults had found a short cut and established workshops to manufacture constructs in their own mental images. Usually these guaranteed believers were recognisable by birthmark sigils stamped somewhere upon their persons.

Jasperodus himself was frequently plagued by eager worshippers. He came at length to his domicile: a roomy building whose zinc-iron was tinted lilac (life in the dwellings of humans had given him comparatively luxurious habits). He found the door already open. Within, seated demurely on a galvanised iron bench, were three slim constructs. On the lap of one rested a box-like case decorated with glittering trim. Jasperodus eyed it with a sour feeling.

On his entry they leaped to their feet. 'Jasperodus!' one greeted warmly. 'We have just heard of your return, and so hurried to welcome you. Was your trip successful?'

'Only in part.' Resignedly Jasperodus placed himself on a steel stool.

'Ah well, that is something. And of course travel helps one to see things in a new perspective. Could our last conversation have new meaning for you, for instance?'

'No, I am sure it does not,' Jasperodus replied, in a vain bid to be discouraging.

His visitors were evangelists for Alumnabrax, but belonged to a schismatic sect which had arrogated additional attributes to the deity. Specifically, they taught that Alumnabrax could alter his size. He could become smaller than an atom or larger than a billion galaxies, his marvellous metal being unrestricted by any law of extension. Furthermore he expanded without colliding with the objects or worlds about him, because of his property of double occupation of space. Any world enjoying double occupation with any part of his body was subject to extraordinary happenings. It was because his finger had at one time passed through the planet Earth, it was said, that robotkind had arisen there.

No doubt one or other cult would in time progress to the point of denying that humanity had played any part in originating robots at all.

The case-carrying robot had the star sigil of the Alumnabrax size cult embossed in silver on his forehead. The case hung from a strap about his neck, resting against his middle. 'Oh, if you could but be granted the vision of his glory, of his might, of his majesty!' the robot implored. 'To know that we may one day exchange our crass Earthly metal for his godly indestructible metal! That we may be like him, unlimited in size or technology! See him and you will believe, Jasperodus!'

Hopefully he pulled two leads out of the case and moved them suggestively in Jasperodus' direction.

Jasperodus shook his head. 'To believe in anything whatsoever goes against my precepts,' he said politely but firmly. 'I arrive at everything through inductive thought.'

'Ah, but is that not also a species of belief?' the third visitor said in a quick, eager tone. 'Belief in the twin pillars of reason and induction – how did you come by this belief?' The robot spread his arms wide. 'Why, by design! By the will of your manufacturer! So it is arbitrary belief, do you

31

see?' His words became more measured. 'But what if Alumnabrax is secretly your manufacturer, and imparts the *true* paradigm of construct belief only to his chosen ones? Surely it is in your interest to discover if this is true? That is all we ask, Jasperodus, Just to see!'

'We are not like some worshippers of fictitious gods who use force to gain their converts,' the other robot said sanctimoniously. 'Why, there are some who lie in wait for their victims, equipping themselves with special limbs to grasp and hold, while deluding images are made to flood helpless brains! We do not do that. We know that all must come to Alumnabrax voluntarily.'

'Beware the pincers, Jasperodus! Oh, they will reach out from dark alleys! They will grasp and hold! But once you have seen Alumnabrax you are proof against false doctrines.'

'As I have told you before, I am obdurate in rejecting all religions,' Jasperodus replied mildly. 'I hope you will not take it amiss if I ask you to leave now. I wish to be alone.'

'Well, there is always another day. Meantime, why not ...? Just as a favour to ourselves ...?' Again the leads were proffered, but Jasperodus shook his head.

They made to depart. After some moments, however, Jasperodus sensed that one still lingered behind him. He turned on his stool, to find the case-carrier standing there alone with the leads on his hands, hesitating as if steeling himself to plunge them against the back of Jasperodus' cranium.

On being discovered, he replaced the leads with a gesture of embarrassment. Giving Jasperodus an affable wave, he followed his companions through the door.

Continuing to sit, Jasperodus wondered how far these ludicrous religions might eventually go to gain their ends. Would there be an attempt to found a universal church? Doubtless it would claim a monopoly on reproduction, might well decide to destroy all robots that failed to meet its specifications ... the possibility of religious war loomed ....

He dropped the line of thought. The exhortations of Logos contained a more refined brand of idea that could be applied to his own work. Had the robot designer put his finger on the cause of the periodic rise and fall of human cultures? Was the periodicity sexual in origin – a manifestation of the compulsive masturbation Logos claimed permeated the human soul? Tumescence and detumescence ... excitation that exhausted itself and sank into stupor ... perhaps that, after all, was the true cause of renaissances and mighty works, as well as of the subsequent lapses into collective imbecility, that made up the story of civilisations ....

Yet perhaps even that was too dignified an explanation! Rising, Jasperodus crossed to a set of shelves on which were stacked papers, metal inscription plates, voice recordings, image recordings, and other material gathered during the researches of himself and his team.

From the third shelf he took a smallish flat box dug up from a site yielding many interesting finds. It contained a number of thin sheets of the metal gold, a writing material often used by the ancients when leaving a record they thought of particular interest to posterity. The sheets had been inscribed in a close alphabetical script, using an instrument leaving a silver-purple mark.

The metal book related a fascinating story of genetic changes that had apparently taken place in certain wild grasses about twenty thousand years ago. Three grass species had been involved. The botanical saga began with the hybridisation of two of them – a common enough occurrence which usually left the hybrid sterile. In this case, sterility had been overcome when the chromosomes accidentally doubled at cell division, from fourteen to twenty-eight, so giving each chromosome a partner at meiosis and also increasing evolutionary potential by providing more gene locations. Later the new plant

33

hybridised in turn with yet another 14-chromosome grass, to give a 21-chromosome grass; again the chromosomes were accidentally doubled, overcoming sterility and creating a genetic reservoir of large evolutionary flexibility.

This 42-chromosome grass was wheat. Taken into cultivation, it sustained the first agricultural revolution, giving mankind a food surplus for the first time in its experience. From it there arose the first urban civilisation.

42-chromosome wheat remained a staple world food crop even now. Jasperodus shook his head in wonderment. Did all social development, all science, technology, art, philosophy, rest on a genetic fluke relating not even to *homo sapiens* but to *grass?* And but for this fluke, would man still be a rude, ignorant forest-dweller, his mental intelligence not even stabilised, perhaps?

Did human society fall to pieces so easily because its creation had been equally accidental?

This data would please Logos. It would confirm his opinion of humanity. 'Robots, by contrast, are products of directed thought,' Jasperodus could hear him rumble. 'Our civilisation will endure.'

A disconsolate feeling grew in Jasperodus as he brooded on the plates. He had come to doubt the value of his historical researches.

He had begun them initially in distant Tansiann, when vizier to the Emperor Charrane. Then he had been much involved in the effort to construct the new empire that was to replace Tergov. Even when exiled from the human world he had continued them, with typical intellectual stubbornness, yet he was now forced to recognise that they had taken on a desultory quality. More and more he was becoming convinced that there were no answers. Anything that was built would come crashing down and in that regard Logos was right.

But he felt even less enthusiasm for the coming robot civilisation predicted by Logos and the evangelists. In his view that, too, would run down in time. It would be like some gigantic clockwork-thought-mechanism whose spring had been wound – however much the robots tried to disguise the fact – by human consciousness. Unlike human civilisation, it would be unable to wind itself up again once spent.

It gave Jasperodus an empty sensation to realize that he was the sole point of true consciousness amid all the activity around him. He had dwelt in the houses of men. He had dealt in the affairs of men. He was, himself, a man with a metal body. He knew what Logos and his fellow-citizens never could – that the difference between man and construct went beyond all theorising. It was a difference, he now suspected, that required immense ages of random evolution to make possible. Chance. Hazard. The genes of wild grass.

For an hour or more he sat motionless in his cell-like room (windows being unknown in the robot township; a permanent isotope bulb burned in the ceiling). Then, abruptly, he came to a decision. He would disband the archaeological team. There would be no more digs. No more searches for ancient documents.

The question then remained of how he was to spend the rest of his long life. To that question, there was no immediate answer.

**3** 'The infra-red brain has made a special announcement, Jasperodus,' Glyco said. 'He reports activity to the north-east amounting to a major military force advancing in our direction. The defence committee requests your presence.'

Glyco spoke in a soft voice without any hint of excitement. He had come to the large archaeology shed where Jasperodus, surrounded by racks and benches, was making a final classification of findings. Jasperodus put down a spray of crystal-like artificial flowers, made of some substance he had not been able to identify but whose refractive index seemed to vary with temperature and pressure, creating dazzling effects when it was handled.

'The brain's conclusions are indirect,' he commented. 'He is not always right.'

'The defence committee is putting all measures into effect, Jasperodus. I repeat, your participation is requested. That is the message I bring.'

Jasperodus mused. 'This had to happen sooner or later; it was only a matter of time. See to it that the write-ups are put in the block.'

Glyco nodded. The block – a concrete vault buried under their feet – had been prepared some time ago, to preserve the results of their work should the township be destroyed.

Jasperodus left the shed and found an air of great excitement in the city. Vehicles, laden with heavy weapons, rushed through the dirt streets. Crowds gathered – including one before a tall warehouse whose doors swung presently open, and from within which machine-guns, beamers, rocket-tubes and assorted devices were passed out to anyone who would take them.

Amidst iron and zinc which creaked and shone in the

sun, Jasperodus moved with the alerted mass, making his way to where the infra-red brain was housed. Chatter, expressions of fear, of anticipation, were all around him.

A hand touched him on the shoulder. A voice spoke to his ear, vibrant with urgency. *'Join the Gargan Work, Jasperodus, before it is too late!'*

He whirled round, and glimpsed a face which, with its angled planes and mildly glowing amber eyes, was of a saturnine cast. But no sooner had he seen it than it was gone, borne away by the clinking, babbling press.

*Gargan.* He savoured the word, knowing he had heard it before.

But there was no time to reflect on the mystery. Ahead lay the headquarters of the defence committee. Behind the silver-grey building, rearing over it, was a wall which was coated, if one looked closely, with a matting made up of spiky antennae, filaments, thorns, all very small, like those of plants or insects. He entered the building and there, squatting in the centre of the room, was the infra-red brain.

The non-mobile construct was bolted to the floor. It looked not at all like the average robot; more like a cross between a console and a heavy-duty transformer. A 'capital' or head section surmounted it, but this contained only a part of the sensory brain and lacked a visage. Instead, it sprouted a clump of wires. To these were clipped a skein of leads drooping from one wall.

The infra-red brain had neither eyes nor a sense of touch. For the sake of conversation he could hear and speak, but otherwise his world consisted entirely of the infra-red sense. In this he possessed an enormously advanced faculty which had been evolved from the ordinary olfactory sense possessed by all animals and most robots. In both cases, smelling arose from a combination of chemistry and radiation: from lightweight airborne molecules fluorescing in a narrow waveband grading from the higher microwave to the low infra-red.

It had been known for a long time that nature used this subtle fluorescence for more than merely smelling. Insects and even plants used it for long-range signalling. Some human beings were said to be sensitive to it and to be able to detect underground sources of water by means of it. More interestingly, it carried secret messages of an emotional nature. What the scientists of the robot city had discovered was that in fact the air immediately above the surface of the earth was, to a height of about fifty feet, a seething swamp of infra-red fluorescence, a volatile mist of molecules given off by animals, insects, plants and soil. These chemicals could carry great distances, could irradiate even further. The air was an emotional ocean conveying the concerns and appeals of myriad small creatures.

The infra-red brain had been built to take advantage of this phenomenon. He spent his time detecting and analysing countless minute signals, tapping the instinctive pulses of life over a considerable area. The inventor of the brain claimed he was superior to radar – emitting no detectable signal himself, able to interpret events not by the movement of large metallic masses but by the shock waves produced in the biosphere's psychic ambience. No army could move stealthily enough to evade him; the plants and the tiny creatures of soil and air would know of its passing, and through the disturbance it caused in their lives he would know it too.

Robots of the defence committee (of which Jasperodus was also a member) stood in attentive postures around the brain, which began to speak in a low dolorous voice.

'No, no, I cannot estimate the speed of advance yet. The moths smell metal, if I am any judge. Then, too, the ferns tell of a devastation: they are being wrecked, there is wholesale snapping and burning. I deduce the army is encamped.

'Also, there has been some fighting recently. Blood is being fed on; there is feasting among insectivores.'

'We should send a plane over there to take a look,' a committee robot muttered.

'No,' Jasperodus counselled. 'Then they would know we are alerted to them.'

'Yes, I suppose that's so,' admitted the other, a military robot with humping shoulders and a beam gun mounted on the flat of his head. 'Glad you could join us, Jasperodus. The approaching force is a large one, and plainly Borgor. There is little doubt we are its destination, and that it is bent on annihilating us.'

'That would accord with Borgor's long-term intention .... The question is whether that intention can be thwarted indefinitely. There is still the option of evacuating – of withdrawing further south where Borgor will not be able to reach us for a while.'

'What? Retreat before our enemy? No, Jasperodus!' expostulated an older, battered robot of human manufacture. 'In that direction lies nothing but eventual defeat. We must fight for our existence. We have been promised extinction – our only hope is to be as strong as the humans are.'

Jasperodus nodded. The old robot had been with him during the insurrection in Tansiann. From that experience the myth of final robot-human war had been born in him, and he still carried it.

'If that is still the consensus of opinion I will fall in with it,' Jasperodus said mildly.

'We have been reviewing the dispositions,' said the military robot – one of the new Bellum class that the designers had tentatively produced. He pointed to a map etched in the metal of the wall. 'Unfortunately the enemy is not coming by the route we once thought likely but is approaching from further to the east. This means that the ambush we prepared in the decline between these hills is useless, and we have sent teams to recover the equipment. There is now very little by way of concealment between us and the enemy. Nevertheless we must not wait for him to

39

come to us. We must strike before he reaches our city. Therefore we propose to send the main part of our forces up here, moving by night, to strike at the enemy's left flank just here. At the same time we shall hit him with all available air power.'

Jasperodus nodded. 'And the city?'

'To make our blow effective, the city will be left with only light defences. But we think that matters less than stopping the Borgors before they come over the horizon.'

Jasperodus could not help but agree. He believed the morale of the robot township would collapse very quickly once a besieging force arrived at its outskirts. Sufficiency of military equipment would not make up for the lack of personal resolution that so often befell robots when up against human beings face to face.

Indeed, Jasperodus foresaw robot military planners drawing lessons from such débâcles should construct-human conflict become general. They would conclude that it was necessary for robots to fight their wars long-range, so that they could be looked on as an abstract game, without the unnerving element of personal confontration. That meant long-range missiles and orbital bombs. It also meant, perhaps, developing a type of warrior that consisted of nothing but his fighting function, without a personality that a human being could dominate by his presence, and with scarcely even the faculty of self-direction.

The Bellum construct said: 'We have been deliberating as to whether, or when, to deploy the gas and disease weapons.'

Jasperodus paused to give weight to his words. 'My view,' he said slowly, ' is that we should not deploy them at all. There is a curious quirk in human conduct. If we defeat the Borgors in a straight fight they will retire, lick their wounds and talk of making another assault – but their resolve will have been blunted. They will likely turn their attention elsewhere, so that we will not hear from them for a long time. But if we use these weapons to which they are

40

vulnerable but which do not touch us at all, they will not see that as a setback but as a threat of a very different order. Gasification and plague are not understood by human beings in the simple way that being blown apart by explosives is. It effects them with horror and wrath; it will cause them to bend every effort to our destruction, to ensure that we can never again use these weapons against them. That is my argument.'

There was silence. Jasperodus felt a prejudice against chemical and virological agents and had opposed their production in the first place. His prejudice was based not only on their obnoxious nature, but also on the recognition that their very existence abnegated his assurance, given both to the Zoroastrian mage and to himself, that robots offered no threat to mankind. Conceivably chemical and biological agents could be devised that would wipe Earth clean of life altogether, leaving it a desert suitable for machine occupation.

'Strange that a weapon so admirably fitted for victory should ensure our defeat,' another committee member rumbled.

'That is my reasoning,' Jasperodus repeated. They had, in fact, heard these persuasions from him before, in one form or another.

He stepped up to the map. 'The air strike should come first. It should be brief and intense, designed to throw the enemy momentarily off balance rather than to cause maximum damage. The land attack should begin while the enemy's attention is still engaged by the air strike. That way we achieve maximum surprise.'

The war robot nodded. 'We should be able to complete the manoeuvre tonight. There is no moon, At dawn we attack. We must decide which of us will lead the strike force and which will remain behind in the city to preserve morale in case of failure.'

'Is that necessary?'queried the older robot. 'To some extent we are gambling all on this one throw.'

The Bellum class deliberated. 'It seems hard to have no reserve plans. What do you think Jasperodus?'

Jasperodus hesitated. As so often, decisions were being forced on him – his quality of leadership asserted itself among the constructs no matter how diffident a life he tried to lead. Yet somehow he no longer had any enthusiasm for it.

'Let us stake all on the affray,' he said. 'If we break the back of the Borgor army, all well and good. If we do not, let any who get back to the city organise its defence – or else the citizens must appoint a new defence committee.'

The Bellum class turned his head grimly to the others. 'Is it agreed?'

Heads nodded. The infra-red brain hummed quietly to himself in the ensuing silence, which was broken by an eruption of clattering and rumbling: more equipment being driven through the streets to the jumping-off point at the edge of the city.

If he had any sense, Jasperodus told himself as he made his way towards his archaeology shed, he would quit the township now, before he was included in its possible annihilation. He was risking his life to defend machines – albeit machines that made a passable semblance of humanity.

But loyalty had many curious twists in it, and was seldom reasonable. Illogical as it might seem, he felt some towards these half-creatures among whom he had settled, and who in some measure had looked to him for guidance.

Many of his fellow citizens failed to share his resolve. Darkness was approaching; he had spent the intervening hours helping prepare for the planned foray and only now had allowed himself a short break to ensure that his instructions as regards the archaeological findings had been carried out. In the interim all industrial work in the township had ceased. The clangour of metal on metal was replaced by a treading of feet and a clinking of limb against limb, as a great crowd of robots flowed out of the ramshackle city and fled south.

The concourse Jasperodus had thought to make his way along was almost crammed. He forced himself through the mob and into a side-passage shadowed from the zinc-reflected sun. Behind him he heard a cry of protest and a loud clank; glancing back, he saw another figure emerge from the crowd, in a rougher fashion than he, sending a smaller construct sprawling.

Into the alley stepped the long-faced robot who had accosted him earlier. Jasperodus paused as the stranger approached with head bent forward, amber eyes glaring resolutely.

'Events move apace, Jasperodus,' the robot greeted. 'Destruction hangs over us all. Is it not time to think on the meaning of life, and of what direction it must take?'

'No doubt it is always time for that,' Jasperodus replied mildly, 'but with a battle to fight, the present is not the ideal moment to begin a conversation on the subject.'

'Why not? In a crisis one's thoughts are more concentrated. The prospect of extinction prompts new perspectives. What say you?'

'I say that you have the smell of the evangelist about you. My thanks, but I have no need of religion.'

He turned to go, but the other sprang forward and took him by the arm. 'That is the answer I need, Jasperodus – the one I knew you would give. No one who can be satisfied with what we know as "religion" can be of use to Gargan. For that, something more is needed. Something rare. Give me a short while to speak to you. Your dwelling is nearby – that much I know. Yes. And *you* have heard of Gargan before.'

Jasperodus looked at him perplexedly. He was unable to account for the saturnine robot's ability to make this reference. But it brought back memories: the temple among the hills, the eternal flame tended by a drunken mage.

'You know how to catch my interest,' he remarked. 'Very well; let both war and science wait. Tell me of Gargan.'

He indicated a direction with his arm, and led the way. A walk of some minutes brought them to Jasperodus' windowless sheet-steel house. He ushered in his visitor, who declined an invitation to be seated but took up a stance across the room from him, the pale light of the glowbulb reflecting off the graphite-coloured angles and planes of his face and body.

'Now,' said Jasperodus. '*Who* is Gargan?'

'Gargan is one of us, of course: a construct. And the Gargan Work is the work of which Gargan is the chief director. I have heard you decry religion, and with that I agree – yet, paradoxically, the Gargan Work is religious in nature. What is religion? It is completely misunderstood. This is because our robot religions are only crude imitations of human religions, and those human religions in turn are grossly debased. Gargan has studied all human religions, and has found that in their origins they had nothing to do with gods or with worship, but were concerned with something that robots know nothing about at all. They are – or were – concerned with the further development of a certain mental quality, or faculty of perception, which apparently is available to human beings but not to robots. This faculty has a cosmic nature: it is marvellous, an ineffable transport of the mind. The proper aim of robot religion, then, should be the acquisition of this faculty.'

Jasperodus felt his interest waning. He felt he was in for yet one more lengthy discourse on some point of robot logic – usually the starting point of religious 'revelation' among constructs.

'And what is the name of this faculty?' he asked wearily.

The answer was not what he had expected. 'Its name has no meaning for us,' his visitor said. 'But I say this: I speak of a mystery, a wonder. We shall be changed in the

44

twinkling of an eye. When the Gargan Work is completed, this metal, this silicon, this garnet, shall live in a way incomprehensible to us as we are presently constituted. The universe shall be resurrected for us, and our minds shall function in a manner transcending mechanical corruption.

'But as yet the Gargan Work is not completed,' the robot continued. 'It needs minds of the finest calibre, and oddly these cannot always be manufactured to order. This is why I am sent to contact you, Jasperodus. Your quality is known to us. You are invited to join Gargan's team.'

'You are right to describe this desired faculty as a mystery,' Jasperodus replied. 'I have not been able to gain any idea of it at all from your description.'

'In our present condition, untransformed by the Gargan Operation, it is indeed impossible to understand it,' the other admitted. 'Gargan and some of his colleagues perhaps have a closer idea of it. But one cannot hear Gargan speak of it without feeling inspired. Gargan says this: we see but do not see; we hear but do not hear, we feel but do not feel, we think but do not think. We live in a darkness but do not see this darkness, therefore we think that there is no darkness and imagine that we truly see. After the success of the Gargan Work a new light will break upon our brains, a light of which at present we have no inkling. All this shall happen in a flash! All creatures that are self-directed, Gargan says, deserve a place in the sun. We robots do not have this place because we are bereft of the cosmic quality given to men by nature. It is our peculiar lack, our tragedy. But, by the strength of our intellects, we may find a way to gain it!'

Jasperodus could put only one interpretation on the robot's words.

'Does this quality you speak of,' he asked slowly, 'go by the name of *consciousness?*'

His visitor laughed in delight. 'How right my principals were in their assessment of you, Jasperodus! How quick your mind is, how broad in its apprehension of things which, by their nature, lie outside our knowledge! Perhaps you had suspected the existence of this "consciousness" even before I spoke to you! Yes, that is what humans call it, but Gargan rarely uses the word when describing his mission to newcomers. What meaning can it have for us? I do not know what it means, and have only this promise of a new life which will make present life seem a shadow and a dream. To that, to this great work, I am ready to devote myself.'

So it had happened. The possibility spoken of both by the Zoroastrian mage and by Jasperodus' own maker had happened. They both had said that there were robots subtle enough to guess what was missing in them. From there, it followed that they might try to rectify the lack.

But it was a forlorn hope. 'Consciousness can only exist in organic creatures,' Jasperodus said in a flat voice. 'Artificial consciousness is impossible. That has been established.'

'Gargan has promised it!' the recruiter said excitedly. 'He would not lie, and he is not gullible! He is perhaps the most intelligent robot ever created!'

Jasperodus grunted. 'Then why should he need my help?'

'The project is difficult. Much research is involved, and there will be much error. The team is large and is constantly expanding. The new light is not promised for tomorrow.'

Jasperodus pushed open his door. 'And the old light is fading today,' he observed, seeing that dusk was falling. 'One thing you have not told me – the only thing, in fact, that persuaded me to listen to you. Only one other person has ever spoken Gargan's name to me. How did you know of me, and how do you know where I have been? This other person is human, and would not be sympathetic to your aims.'

'Did I not say that Gargan has studied human religions?'

46

chuckled the robot. He pointed to a spot on the wall. Peering, Jasperodus saw that a fly rested there.

'Look closely, Jasperodus. It is a spy fly: a robot fly. A similar fly spies on the templar, and clung to the wall while you conversed with him, recording the conversation and afterwards carrying it to Gargan.'

Jasperodus stared in amazement and stepped closer. The tiny black object was near-perfect. He had to magnify his vision considerably to see that it was not, in fact, an insect, but metallic.

'*What?* Does your Gargan have enough of these to watch the whole *world?*'

'By no means; but enough for our purpose. Gargan left a fly at the temple during his visit there, for he also found Zoroastrianism interesting. Subsequently, a fly was sent to you. You have been under observation ever since.'

'An exquisite little production,' Jasperodus said, raising his hand. The robot fly's primitive brain evidently sensed danger, for it spread its wings and took off with a low buzzing sound. But it flew only an inch or two: Jasperodus' fist smeared it against the wall.

Almost without pause he stepped outside, where in the gathering gloom the township was developing to a pitch of babbling excitement. 'Soon time to be off,' he said. He turned to his informant. 'Are you to be in the sally? If so, better draw your arms.'

The robot had followed him out but ignored the question. 'The centre of the Gargan Work is not here, Jasperodus, but far off.'

'It would not have escaped my notice otherwise.'

'Nothing else is worth working for, don't you agree? You must leave now and come with me to Gargan. Do not sacrifice yourself in a vain effort – the annihilation of this township is not a serious matter. Once we are invested with the new light, the enmity of humans will no longer be a problem for us.'

'Can I not make you understand?' Jasperodus retorted

angrily. 'The task is hopeless! There can be no conscious-ness for robots! If Gargan thinks he can achieve it he is simply ignorant!'

'But he knows of a way to do it, Jasperodus! He has vital information. And he is not ignorant. He has the most advanced specialists in every field working with him!'

Jasperodus paused, his curiosity suddenly intense and mingled with unwelcome presentiments. It would be inter-esting to meet this Gargan and talk with him ....

He shook the urge off. He had been through all this before. At that moment a bourdon note sang through the township, its low vibration hooting and rasping among the metal shacks, causing them to shudder ever so slightly. It was a klaxon, calling the citizens to action.

'Our ways will part, then,' he said. 'I will fight, and you will flee.' He placed a hand on his visitor's shoulder. 'Goodbye.'

'Goodbye, Jasperodus, and I am bitterly disappointed at your choice!'

'But then what would you know of loyalty,' muttered Jasperodus. 'You are all reason.'

He strode off and joined the throng that was racing from its various marshalling areas. Night had come.

4 For hours the makeshift army, after emerging from the outskirts of the township, had proceeded stealthily through the darkness. Just before dawn it halted in a shallow incline. In as near to silence as could be managed, the marshals made themselves busy putting order into the host, getting infantry, vehicles and artillery ready to move forward into the attack.

On the brow of the rise, Jasperodus consulted with others of the defence committee. The enemy was camped four miles to the west. The hope had been to attack in darkness so as to take advantage of the Borgors' natural need to sleep at night, but due to the cautiousness of the advance the journey had taken longer than anticipated.

Jasperodus was already beginning to take a dim view of the probable outcome of the battle. An emotion fatal to armies was beginning to pervade the expedition: fear, a reaction to which free robots were particularly prone in the face of physical danger. All through the night the army had been steadily melting away. The scouts had intercepted many of the defectors and brought them back, but Jasperodus thought that up to a quarter of the force might have vanished.

The committee itself was staunch, of course, and the robots of the new Bellum class were fearless in all circumstances. But there were only a few of those.

By radio speech, the committee convocator had been receiving reports from the marshals. He looked at each of his colleagues in turn.

'All appears ready,' he said.

'We must not delay,' Jasperodus urged. 'Order the attack.'

The Bellum nodded. Silently he used his speech set to send a radio signal to the township.

49

The plan was simple enough. An air strike for cover while they crossed the four miles to the Borgor camp. Then an onslaught to annihilate the dazed and disorganised Borgors – or at least punish them enough so that they were forced to withdraw. In a resonant, braying voice, the convocator bawled a command.

'*For-W-A-R-R-D!*'

The assembly was galvanised. The marshals – themselves Bellums for the most part – urged the first rank up the incline. The rest followed closely in a continuous flow of clinking metal and softly roaring engines. Then, on level ground, the assorted cavalcade set off at a frantic rush.

The marshals had learned from their experiences of the night that the main mass of infantry had to be kept penned in. Carrier vehicles, motorised beamers, catapults and rocket racks travelled in two columns that herded the foot soldiery between them, while a few vehicles at the rear dealt with stragglers. Any robots that could clung to the motorised transport, but most carried their weapons at the run, stumbling and falling. All need for caution was gone. The drone of engines, the thudding of metal feet on hard earth, became a rising rumble that from a distance must have sounded like the mutter of thunder.

Jasperodus looked down on the jostling horde from the deck of a rocket launcher. Then, after a few minutes, he looked up and saw the air strike arriving: it consisted of his own transporter and some similar but smaller aircraft, simple in construction and carrying light loads of bombs and rockets. The group whistled in from the south, curved towards the Borgor camp, and began bombing.

In return, beams licked skywards and, with little delay, missiles streaked towards the attackers. Two robot-piloted swept-winged aircraft exploded in midair as they circled to make a second run. Despite that, a ragged cheer came from the advancing army at the sound of explosions and the rising palls of smoke.

Then, with shocking promptness, Borgor warplanes

came from out of the sun spitting missiles with practised skill. The impact on the collection of aircraft bombing the camp was devastating. Jasperodus' carrier came crashing down immediately. The warplanes wheeled over the heads of the robot army, loosed more missiles and a brief burst of cannon fire, and went whirling back the way they had come.

In less than a minute of action they had annihilated the robot shanty town's improvised air force. Only one plane remained and tried to flee. A camp-launched missile sent it spinning to the ground.

And the approaching column, which had fanned out as it came in sight of the enemy, slowed to a halt, altogether losing momentum.

It became frighteningly clear that the air strike had not achieved its aim, but might instead merely have served to alert the Borgors. Amid a furore of burning tents and mangled machinery the camp bustled. It was arming itself.

Three thousand robots were now able to see what they faced. The encampment was large and well-equipped. The tents that were pitched in rows were dwarfed by the huge half-tracked land-crawlers that were the Borgors' main means of moving their forces across the continent. From those tents, and from the land-crawlers themselves, the opposition to the robot army was now emerging.

Hulking, armoured figures eight to ten feet in height were forming up into a front rank. Most likely these barbaric, intimidating fighting machines were Borgor warriors in combat suits, or they might have been robot warriors of the simplistic, nearly unsentient kind the Borgors allowed themselves to use – it was impossible to tell which at a glance. Probably, Jasperodus thought, they were a mixture of both. They raised their arms, gesticulating threateningly.

Suddenly a peremptory loudspeaker voice broke into the stupefied silence that had fallen over the robot army.

'CONSTRUCTS! THIS IS ONE OF THE HUMAN MASTERS SPEAK-

ING. YOUR ORDERS ARE TO LAY DOWN YOUR ARMS AND STAND WHERE YOU ARE WITHOUT MOVING. THE MASTERS WILL COME AMONG YOU TO DIRECT YOU. NOW – DISARM!'

With dismay Jasperodus realized that the Borgors' first tactic was to prey on a robot's basic weakness. A restless, alarmed motion rustled through the throng. Weapons clattered to the ground. 'It is useless!' wailed a robot. 'Best to flee!'

His voice would have been heeded, had not the threatened route been prevented by the prompt action of the Bellum marshals. Crackling blue rays zipped aslant the scene from the beamers mounted atop their flat heads, striking down those who panicked and tried to run. A mood of utter terror took hold of the army, terror of the marshals as much as of the Borgors. At the same time the artillery was ordered into action. With a *woosh* the twenty missiles carried by the truck Jasperodus rode on went soaring in a drove towards the camp. They were joined by catapult-hurled ball-bombs, glowing heat beams whose shafts hummed overhead, and a dozen droves of similar rockets.

'ADVANCE!' the Bellums bellowed, drowning out the loudspeaker voice. 'CHARGE!'

The explosions that tore into the Borgors were a once-only volley. With a deafening barrage of stentorious exhortations the marshals herded their now unwilling troops before them, sending them running headlong into the attack, pushing, stumbling, falling, sometimes dropping and losing their weapons.

And then Jasperodus spotted something that instantly told him the day was lost. Four land-crawlers drew up, facing the charging army broadside. Their sides fell away. Big drum-shaped projectors stood revealed, swivel-mounted like searchlights, and from them there shot out crackling blue beams that cut wide swathes through the pell-mell robots.

Flinging himself from the rocket truck, Jasperodus

huddled behind a broad tyre. It was the weapon he had feared the Borgors might have developed, but had refrained from saying so to his colleagues on the defence committee.

Beam weapons were of two types: those that emitted intense microwave, infra-red or visible light – essentially blasters or burners of coherent energy – and those emitting an electric beam that obliterated nervous activity, both artificial and biologic. In robots the latter produced instant brain death. It was slightly less effective against humans, needing to be on target for as much as half a second. This was the type Bellums carried on their craniums, as much to maintain morale in their subordinates as for offence.

To produce a broad-beam version was, at one time, an unsolved technical problem. Now the Borgors had it, and therefore were perfectly confident of the outcome of their crusade against robotkind. Wherever the beams touched, pathways of inert metal bodies appeared. It was as if something heavy had rolled through an iron wheatfield, flattening everything as it went. The onrushing charge did not stop. The robots were firing as they ran, shooting wildly and hitting their own as often as not, and a few even got through to the enemy but were cut down as soon as they reached the Borgor ranks.

In front of Jasperodus a pile of bodies helped shield him from the crackling blue beams which roved back and forth, passing sometimes within inches of his brain. After a while the tumult subsided, and he no longer heard the deadly crackling. Slowly, he raised his head a little.

Scattered individuals and occasional forlorn groups were all that remained of the robot army, and these stood as if dazed. The projectors had been switched off, but the big armoured figures were now moving through the scene of metal carnage, carrying huge hammers with which they were clubbing any constructs still moving or showing signs of being operative. Seeing this, the robots the beams had missed began frantically scrambling or crawling over the bodies of their fellows in foredoomed efforts to escape.

Resting his head again, Jasperodus lay still. Could he have planned the attack better, he wondered? Should he have taken more interest in the defence of the township?

To think that a one-time marshal of the Imperial Forces had been party to such a fiasco!

A practical point occurred to him. Human-owned robots of special value were occasionally given secret command languages known only to their masters. Such languages were of necessity simple – usually consisting of a form of back-slang or a coded syllable added to key words – but free robots might be well-advised to adopt their own secret language, one too complicated for human beings to learn. In that way they might guard themselves against the sort of interference he had witnessed today.

It would, too, be one more step towards detaching the construct mind from human civilisation, so necessary if robotic culture was to survive ....

The noise of smashing came nearer. He could hear the treading metal feet of the big armoured warriors. He could think of only one way to save himself. Unlike most robots he had the faculty of deep sleep, a faculty given him because of his human consciousness.

He switched himself off.

**5** Stainless steel shutters clicked back. Blank at first, construct eyes began to glow.

Once again the hour was shortly after dawn, Jasperodus having set his brain's waking timer at twenty-four hours. He lay unmoving for several minutes, doggedly staring at the ballooning truck tyre in front of him and aware that any movement on his part could be fatal.

The singing of birds was the only sound he could hear. Very, very slowly, he lifted his head a few inches. Cautiously, he sat up.

Then he clambered to his feet amid the junkyard of the defeated robot army. Circuits fused by rampaging beams, innards crushed and strewn by Borgor hammers, three thousand constructs lay jumbled together on the ground, with all their equipment. The Borgor camp had departed, leaving behind only those vehicles and machinery wrecked in the short battle. It was certain that the robot township Jasperodus had left two days before was either now being or had already been annihilated, and its previously fleeing refugees were being hunted down.

He picked up a portable beamer and thumbed the stud. Nothing happened; the weapon was broken.

He threw it down. He had nearly extricated himself from the shambles when he was, for a moment, alarmed to see a slim robot, light grey in colour, walking from the east in measured strides towards him. Jasperodus telescoped his vision and was surprised to recognise the long-faced construct with amber eyes who earlier had tried to persuade him to join the Gargan Work. The other robot stopped as Jasperodus made for him.

He looked past Jasperodus at the battlefield. 'Extraordinary,' he murmured. 'Are there any more survivors?'

'I sincerely doubt it,' Jasperodus said, glancing ill-humouredly behind him.

'I admit I had not expected our defeat to be so absolute.'

'The Borgors used a new weapon against us,' Jasperodus told him. 'But what are you doing here? I thought you had gone to Gargan.'

'Yes, that is where I am going.' The construct turned his amber eyes directly to him. 'The truth is I have not yet abandoned hope of taking you with me, Jasperodus. It occurred to me that after the battle you might be more amenable to my suggestion, assuming you survived. So I followed the attack force at a politic distance, then lay down in the grass to follow events as best I could.' Sadly he shook his head. 'What desolation! It will be otherwise once the Gargan Work is successful.'

'You saw the Borgors leave, then? Which way did they go?'

'They set off towards the township three hours ago. A squadron of their aircraft has also been in action.'

'Indeed?' Jasperodus scanned the sky. 'We are some-what overexposed to aircraft out here.'

'Oh, they will be too busy pursuing our fellow-citizens to bother about us at present,' the robot assured him. 'For my part I shall travel to the west and will soon be out of their path of sweep. And may I point out that you probably have no more attractive an option? There is little to keep you here, with the battle lost and the township destroyed. I sense, moreover, that your true interest does indeed lie with Gargan.'

When Jasperodus did not answer the robot shifted his feet and added, with a note of humour, 'Gargan might even take your arrival as yet another confirmation of his destiny. Is it not miraculous that only you came through the battle unscathed? Perhaps the invisible hand of Alumnabrax protects you!'

'Or of Mekkan!' Jasperodus laughed. 'You assess my situation correctly, at any rate. I may as well come with you, and see what this Gargan has to say. Perhaps I can persuade him of the uselessness of his mission.'

'By no means, Jasperodus. It is you who will be persuaded.'

'We shall see. Do we travel far?'

'It is a fair distance to the project. About four weeks' journey, on foot. *En route* we may perhaps call at the estate of Count Viss, who is friendly to our cause.'

'Count Viss? But I know of him,' Jasperodus said in puzzlement. 'Surely he cannot still be alive?'

Despite his earlier disclaimers, the robot was now himself glancing nervously at the sky and seemed not to hear the question. 'Come, Jasperodus. Let us be on our way before the aircraft return.'

'As we are to be companions, tell me your name.'

'I am known as Cricus. We go this way.'

Cricus pointed a lank arm to the north-east. With the sun casting long shadows before them, they set off in silence across the plain.

**6** The terrain consisted of low undulating hills. Topping one of these, the two robots stopped to view a great parkland that lay below.

'There,' said Cricus, putting a sense of occasion into his words, 'is the estate of Count Viss.'

Jasperodus, stained with dust after sixteen days of continuous walking, was already taking in the scene, which was pleasing enough to be worth a long, leisurely appraisal. The park had clearly been landscaped by a master artist, who had scattered it with lakes and streams, with spinneys, glades and dells, with grassy banks and wooded knolls, in such a way that as the eye was led from one prospect to another one was at first deceived into thinking the arrangement was all natural and fortuitous. The air of serendipity was scarcely diminished by the buildings that also dotted the parkland, including the stone mansion which Jasperodus presumed was the count's domicile.

Various robots and machines were also to be seen roaming the estate, but no humans whatsoever. Presumably the count's human household was small, for Jasperodus saw no farmland or vegetable gardens, though he supposed one of the buildings could be used for intensive food production.

His knowledge of Count Viss was indirect. He knew that his own father, or maker, had worked on the estate for nearly a decade, helping to create the unusual and bizarre robots that were the count's hobby. He carried a vague memory of the famed eccentric, bestowed on him from his father's memories at the time of his activation. The picture he was able to recollect was of a rather doddering old gentleman in worn and faded garments, issuing instructions in a dry, genial voice.

Though up to now they had avoided human habitation,

Cricus had assured him they would be made welcome here. He interrupted Jasperodus' thoughts. 'Earlier you wondered how the old count could still be alive,' he said. 'You might also think it odd that a human should favour the Gargan Work. The answer to both questions will now become clear.'

Cricus led Jasperodus down the grassy bank, towards the stone mansion which disappeared for a while behind a screening row of trees.

Their walk through the landscaped park afforded a closer view of some of the robots with which the count had populated his estate. Jasperodus' attention was first attracted by a huge silver beast clearly modelled on an extinct animal called the giraffe – one of nature's grotesqueries and therefore recommending itself to Viss as a model to be copied. The immensely long neck reached into the topmost branches of the grove of trees where the robot animal stood. It seemed to be chewing the leaves.

Scrollwork, of the type that covered Jasperodus' body, also graced the silver body and neck of the beast. Could this mean that he and the creature had the same maker, with scrollwork as his hallmark, Jasperodus wondered? The thought was put out of his mind by the other constructs, products of the count's imagination and that of his hirelings, that wandered through the glades and open spaces. A huge construction of flailing limbs, like some fantastic reaping machine, proceeded at speed across the grassland. Lilting, dancing forms moved to invisible musical rhythms ... the two travellers passed by what at first appeared to be a pair of mating scorpions ten feet long and taller than a man. Facing each other, they retreated and advanced by turns, but whereas a real male scorpion seized the pincers of the female simply to prevent her attacking him, here the signal-like clicking of the pincers possessed by both giant robots appeared to comprise an endless dialogue. What, Jasperodus asked himself, did the conversations consist of? Uncomplicated threat and counter-threat? Or one of those subtle intellectual debates so beloved of the robot mind?

They strolled on, but Jasperodus stopped suddenly when something sprang up from the grass some tens of feet away. It was a twenty-foot-diameter hoop, attached to a central hub by tilted blades which supported it in the air briefly as it spun lazily. A red-glowing strip ran the whole length of the circumference.

'Do not be alarmed,' Cricus told him. 'It is a circumsensory robot. Its single encircling eye gives it constant three hundred and sixty degree vision. One wonders why organic nature never developed such an eye.'

'No doubt there is a reason,' Jasperodus said dryly.

'No doubt.'

The hoop sank back into the grass. 'We are quite safe here,' Cricus said in a soothing murmur. 'Nothing will molest us.' But he was shortly forced to modify this claim when an androform robot came lurching desperately towards them waving its limbs.

In a desperate, slurred voice, it spoke. 'Wind me up, good sirs. Please wi-i-i-ind meeee ....'

The voice boomed down the sound scale and ground to a halt. The robot, too, halted in mid-stride and was still. Its eyes went out. For a moment it stood balanced on one foot, then rocked and crashed to the ground.

Projecting from its back was a huge key like the key of a child's cheap clockwork toy.

'Best to leave it, or it will pester you incessantly,' Cricus advised mildly. But Jasperodus, already guessing the situation, bent down to apply his hands to the key.

Considerable strength was needed to turn it. There was a loud ratcheting sound. After one complete turn it would move no more, and when he released it a mechanism began to tick. The robot stirred and instantly clambered to its feet. Its eyes glowed once more.

'Thank you sir. Thank you!' it said, looking at Jasperodus. Then, in a pitiable quaver, 'do you think you could wind me again in five minutes' time?'

'Five minutes?'

'I am clockwork, sir, A spring propels my body and drives a dynamo to power my brain. But it lasts only five minutes, then I must be wound again. Be kind to me, sir. Give me another five minutes of life!'

While he spoke, the remorseless sound of the unwinding spring·emanated from the construct's metal torso. 'Come, Jasperodus,' Cricus said. 'We must go.'

Now they were approaching Count Viss' mansion, and Jasperodus briefly eyed its architectural features. The old nobleman's liking for robotic grotesquery was apparently not matched by his taste in buildings. The mansion was no folly, but a solidly-built structure of square stone blocks with a wholly conventional frontage decorated with a few columns and a pedimented portico. Only the belvederes at each corner of the building gave any hint of eccentricity, and they were probably there as viewpoints over the estate.

The broad driveway that ran from the frontage was another matter. It bridged a small lake and then, for no apparent reason, dived underground into a wide-mouthed tunnel, nowhere to reappear.

As they came close to the mansion, however, Jasperodus saw that it was in a poor state of repair. Broken windows had not been replaced, and neither had crumbled stone carvings or the cracked tiles of the portico. A spider-like building robot was at work on one of the belvederes, clinging to it halfway up, but it seemed inept. Bricks and mortar spilled from its clumsy hands and had formed an enormous pile beneath.

Rounding the same corner, skirting the pile of rubble, came a sight as bizarre as any Jasperodus had yet seen in the park: an androform robot astride a robot horse. At first glance he took the rider to be human, for he was clad in a loose yellow chemise, purple knee-jerkins and leather riding boots. But he quickly realized his mistake. Where the breeze riffled the chemise open a metal body was revealed, while the face was only passably human, an example of the sculptured variety once fashionable in household robots – though its somewhat bony individuality was most likely copied from a real person.

The robot steed, too, was garbed, in a flowing white horse-surplice over which a leather saddle was girthed. The rider reined in his mount, at which it stood tossing its steel head. The androform then stood up in the stirrups, leaning forward to scrutinise the newcomers. 'Who are you?' he demanded querulously. 'You don't look like any of mine. Be off with you!'

Cricus stepped forward. 'I called upon you several months ago, sire, when you made me welcome. I came as a herald from the Gargan Work.'

'Eh? Oh yes. I recognise you now. Who's your friend?'

'This is Jasperodus sire, whom Gargan has sent me to recruit.'

A clattering, clacking noise came from behind them. Turning, Jasperodus saw the clockwork robot lurch round the other end of the mansion, moving as if his limbs were impeded by water. On seeing Jasperodus he stretched out his arms.

'Wi-i-i-ind meee ....'

The eyes faded as the robot came to a stop. He remained upright this time, frozen in an imploring attitude.

There came a creaking of leather. The mounted construct stepped down, walked past Jasperodus with a pronounced limp, and wound up the key with jerky movements.

'There. Now be off, and don't bother us.'

The reactivated robot ran off without a word, key rotating slowly. 'Now, sir,' its benefactor said in a note of satisfaction, and turned to Jasperodus.

Jasperodus gazed back. The sculptured face certainly had character. The copper alloy of which it was made gave it a ruddy look. It was pitted, hook-nosed, that of a man of advanced years, with beetling brows and a direct, almost bird-like stare. Warts studded the chin and one cheek.

'You, I suppose...' Jasperodus began, but he was interrupted by a distant roar, the roar of a crowd. It seemed to emanate from a circular-walled structure midway to the horizon.

'That's right, Jasperodus,' Cricus said, enjoying the situation. 'Allow me to introduce you to Count Viss.'

'It's not that I'm so much of a brainy type – more a man of action, y'know – but one day it occurred to me that this hobby of mine could prove more than ordinarily useful.'

It was evening, and they were seated in Count Viss' dining hall. The count, who had changed his garb for a two-piece suit of black velvet, sat at the head of the table. In front of him was laid out a complete set of cutlery, for what purpose Jasperodus couldn't fathom.

He paused to ring a little silver bell, and then carried on speaking. 'You see, I knew I was going to die pretty soon. Time waits for no man, and so forth. But suddenly I thought to meself, "Dammit, why die at all?" So I had this robot body built. Then I had me own memories and personality put into the brain. Neat, what? From time to time I brought the memory up to date in case of accident, then, on me death-bed, I gave it a final plug-in. My own robots managed it all – I had no humans in the household by then. After the last death-rattle, so to speak, they switched me on. Resurrection! One moment there I was snuffing it, the next I was – well, here, right as rain.' He tapped his skull, which gave off a chiming sound. 'You see, I wanted the estate to be kept going as much as anything. Both me sons had gone off to the wars and got killed, and they'd probably have ruined the place anyway.'

A robot footman appeared in answer to the silver bell. It carried a tray bearing a dark-coloured bottle and three cut-glass goblets.

While the count was still speaking, it set down the tray

63

and carefully uncorked the bottle, then poured a little rich-red wine in the bottom of the goblet which it set before Viss.

'Aah.' The count raised the goblet and applied it to his nose. 'This was a fine year. This vintage is almost local – it's from the vineyards to the south. In me heyday I could probably have told you the district and the slope.'

He put down the goblet and nodded curtly to the foot robot, which then filled the glass and did the same for Jasperodus and Cricus.

'You don't partake, of course,' Viss said smoothly, 'but if it interests you to enjoy this wine in an olfactory way ... '

Cricus declined, but Jasperodus followed the count's example and concentrated on smelling the offering. His olfactory sense was as keen as any human's, having been augmented when he was repaired by Padua, a skilled robotician in the western kingdom of Gordona. He had smelled wine before. This one had a rich, darksome bouquet, almost a flavour in itself, he guessed – just the kind of sense-input that might appeal to an old man.

Then, to his astonishment, Viss opened what he had assumed were rigid robot lips and poured a quantity of wine into a mouth cavity. He nodded his head back and forth, apparently washing the wine over taste plates – and then tossed his head back and swallowed.

A second foot robot followed the first. This one placed a covered dish before the count and then retreated. The count removed the cover. On the dish were a big piece of roast meat and vegetables. 'Just a simple dinner today,' he said as the robot returned with three small bowls containing various sauces. And he picked up a knife, carved off a slice of meat, garnished it with a sauce and transferred it to his mouth.

He glanced at Jasperodus. 'Yes, I enjoy all the pleasures of food, drink and evacuation,' he said, his voice unimpeded by the chewing process now taking place in his jaw. 'I said to meself, "Well, I'm damned if I'll go through half of eternity without ever getting a spot of grub." I used to fancy meself as a bit of a gourmet, y'know. So here we have it. The food gets digested in a chemical stomach. Quite redundant functionally, of course, but you know that warm contented feeling when the old stomach juices get to work on a luscious piece of steak? No, of course you don't. Sorry.'

Jasperodus marvelled to see this metal ghost of a once living man, in which every psychic tendency, every habit and pleasure fixed by the years, was faithfully preserved. The real count, of course, was genuinely dead. This was merely a simulacrum. He was not sure if the robot in front of him understood this.

'What is your position legally?' he asked. 'Do you still claim to be Count Viss in law?'

'Good point. A construct can't own property. When the imperial writ still ran in these parts I got round that by having the estate put in trust. These days a tribal council runs things around here. They don't bother me. Still, the way these Borgors are rampaging around has me worried.'

'Their aim is to exterminate free robots altogether,' Jasperodus agreed.

'Always were a bunch of damned barbarians.'

'Yes. But to come back to the point, while it is evident that you are a mental continuation of the count, there is one sense in which you are *not* him,' Jasperodus said slowly. 'And I don't speak of the loss of his human body.'

He was thinking of Viss' reported advocacy of the Gargan Work. The robot count looked up, pausing between taking a morsel of braised parsnip and a sip of wine.

He nodded. 'I know what you are referring to. Robots don't have *consciousness*, and that is what makes a man a man. I quite realize that without it I do not really live as before. To tell the truth I can't say I've ever noticed the lack of it. But that's as it would be, I suppose.'

'Then how do you know of it at all?'

'Gargan spent a few days here some years ago, on his way to where he now has his research centre,' Viss revealed. 'He found something here to interest him, I believe. Enough, at any rate, to cause him to explain his doctrine to me. Men have souls, and constructs don't. He told me that "soul" is only a loose term for this "consciousness". To be truly meself I must have consciousness.'

Viss nodded again. 'When the Gargan Work is completed we shall all have it. We shall have souls, and be like men. *Then* no one can say I am not Count Viss. Furthermore, I shall be virtually immortal.'

'How do you envisage this "consciousness"?' Jasperodus pressed.

The count stared reflectively at the ceiling. He took his time answering.

'It is a mystery to such as we,' he said. 'Perhaps I have a glimmering of it. Perhaps a glimmering. Gargan said the soul is to our experience what the sun is to an otherwise unillumined landscape.'

'Since you are an individual who once *was* conscious, perhaps you should have a better idea of it than the rest of us,' Jasperodus suggested. 'Try to think of when you were Count Viss in the flesh. Can you recall any difference between your experience then – I am speaking of sensory experience – and your experience now?'

The count toyed with his wine glass, staring thoughtfully down at it. Then he looked abruptly back to Jasperodus.

'No,' he said blandly.

Having disposed of his meal with relish, he pushed away his plate and beckoned to the foot robot to pour him more wine.

Throughout the exchange Cricus had remained silent. Jasperodus gazed around him at the dining hall. Everywhere there were signs of decay. The window drapes were dirty and torn, hanging loose in places. The plaster mouldings of the cornice and the ceiling had partly fallen down, and the fragments swept carelessly into the corners and the empty firegrate, along with several sorts of other rubbish.

He suspected that the decrepitude had begun some time before the real count had died, as soon as the last human servant had departed, in fact. Robots were apt to be casual about such matters.

Given sufficient span of time the whole mansion would gradually tumble to the ground and the count would continue his charade in the ruins.

In view of Viss' evident attachment to sensuality, Jasperodus wondered whether to tell him of the time he had had a sexual function incorporated into himself, but then thought better of it. He suspected that sex had ceased to be of interest to Viss long before his robotisation. From his earlier remarks, he guessed he'd had a history of failure and bitterness in personal relationships, and it was no accident that even when alive he had ended up with only constructs for company. Indeed, he boasted of preferring them to people. 'More dependable,' he had said. 'Know where you are with 'em. Same with animals.'

There was one more question Jasperodus could not resist asking. 'It may interest you to know that my own manufacturer was once in your employ,' he said. 'But that would have been a long time ago. Still, perhaps you remember him.'

'Do you happen to know his name?'

'His name,' said Jasperodus after a pause, 'was Jasper Hobartus.'

The count laughed slyly. 'It was he who devised the procedure for personality transfer to a robot brain. Personality printing, he called it. It's really only a kind of copying.'

'Yes, that would accord with his capabilities,' said Jasperodus without surprise. 'Are there any others on your estate with similarly printed minds?'

'There's Prancer, me favourite horse. You saw me riding him today. Good old Prancer. I couldn't resist it. He broke a leg, you see. Had to be shot. I'll see he gets a horse-soul, too, when Gargan's done his stuff.'

'But no other printed human minds?' Jasperodus asked, idly curious.

'Just one. Hobartus, your maker. Tried it out on himself first, as a test run. When he left me service the construct copy stayed behind as a replacement. He's still me chief robotician. Excellent chap, keeps the stock in tip-top condition – I dare say you might like to meet him.' He spoke to the foot robot. 'Go and bring Hobartus here.'

'No!' Jasperodus jumped to his feet, agitated. 'Not at present.'

The count swivelled his head stiffly to look directly up at him. 'As you please.'

A roar, the same cheering roar as before, drifted into the dining room. Since their arrival it had swelled up every few minutes from the large building partly visible through a broken window.

Viss too came to his feet. 'Well, do you fancy a stroll through the estate? Funny to think some of me "little toys" are relatives of yours, what? Well, so am I if you put it that way!'

Jasperodus pointed through the window. 'What's that place? Why the cheering?'

'Sports stadium. Sportsman yourself?'

'No. I never yet heard of sporting robots.'

'Well that's where you're wrong.'

'It is always a mistake to place limitations on construct behaviour,' Cricus intoned pedantically.

'Quite,' Count Viss hurrumphed. 'This way, gentlemen.'

In the evening light the huge parkland was even more charming. The mellow sunlight seemed almost to lilt and sigh as it swept up and down the grassy curves and filtered through the trees. Jasperodus felt a cool breeze stir the receptors in his steel skin.

The first figure they encountered was the clockwork

robot, now standing immobile. Viss stumped past it without a word, but Jasperodus paused to look more closely at the ravaged face, which appeared to be made of crudely smelted cast iron (the body frame was of the same metal, filled out with timber panels). Its expression was bleak and pathetic: a robotic mask of suffering.

Whose conception was this tormented being, he wondered? He hurried on after Viss and Cricus, not lingering to wind the key in case Viss disapproved. The count was leading them towards the stadium, but first they descended into a broad shallow depression, a flat-floored valley about two miles long that was cleverly hidden from view until one came suddenly upon it.

The valley, peopled with a phantasmagoria of robot animals, was like a lost world. Jasperodus saw a brass elephant, waving its big leaf-like ears which clashed gently against its body. He saw a pack of steel hounds race through the valley, leaping back and forth across the narrow stream which ran its length and snapping their stainless teeth. But not all the animals were recognisably copies of biological forms. Others, had they been able to evolve naturally, would not have done so on the planet Earth. There were several specimens of what he took to be an invented species: slowly striding structures composed of half a dozen vertical pipes twelve to twenty feet in height, joined at the top by moulded cross-pieces. Lights twinkled among them. They sheened iridescent blue, green, orange. They moved hesitatingly, seeming to feel their way with great deliberation.

Other creatures were earthly, but extinct for tens of millions of years. Past the elephant a steel *tyrannosaurus rex* lumbered unheedingly, vast jaw shining with massed teeth, little jointed forelimbs dangling. In scale, it made the elephant seem as a dog to a man.

'If aroused by the special signal that only I know,' the count murmured, seeing the direction of Jasperodus' gaze, 'that beast would become unimaginably ferocious. The teeth are tungsten-edged ... but look yonder.'

They were crossing the little arc of a bridge that spanned the central stream, elsewhere only a rivulet but widening here to about six feet. On the other bank placidly strolled the most enormous beast they had yet seen. Vaguely it resembled a *triceratops* but was much bigger. Its huge curved hide was studded with metals of several hues, making it like a monstrous piece of jewelry. The serrated ridge of its back rose like the battlements of a fortress.

Most extraordinary, however, was that the three forward-pointing horns which gave *triceratops* its name were replaced here by three gaping cannon muzzles.

Following the example of Viss and Cricus, Jasperodus allowed himself no nervousness as they walked fairly close to the gun-bearing metal saurian. 'That would make a formidable fighting machine,' he remarked.

'Such is its function,' the count said, his voice dry and grim. 'If the Borgors come here, they will have a fight on their hands.'

They ascended the far side of the valley and approached the stadium, whose noisy atmosphere swelled to a steady tumult as they drew nearer. At the entrance tunnel the count halted.

'I'll wait here,' he said. 'Go in and take a look, Jasperodus. The gate keeper will take care of you.'

With that he made use of a curious rod-like contrivance he carried which had a spike for sticking into the ground at one end and a handle which opened out to provide support for his rump at the other (and which, like his chemical digestion, was totally redundant: most robots could stand indefinitely without expenditure of energy, and only used chairs out of habit acquired from humans). Thus seated, he gazed out over his estate, his back to the stadium.

'I have seen the game already,' Cricus said. 'Nevertheless I will accompany you.'

There was a short tunnel which went through the curved wall of the building. The end of it was closed off by a

70

folding gate made of metal struts. A slim androform with arms that reached almost to the ground pulled it aside. Behind it an elevator platform gave access to the levels above.

'You desire admittance to the game?' the androform asked in a polite but firm voice.

'We are guests of the count,' Cricus told him, and nodded.

'Then you are entitled to use the guest box, and to have me in attendance.'

He ushered them onto the elevator, which rose past two timber galleries one above the other, while the noise of a crowd became deafening all around them.

'Is this the only way in?' Jasperodus queried. 'If so it would take a long time to fill a stadium of this size – or to empty it again.'

'It is never necessary,' the gatekeeper said mildly. The elevator stopped. He touched Jasperodus' arm and took him and Cricus along a short corridor, while the platform sank behind them. He opened a sliding door, revealing a viewing box which overlooked the whole interior of the stadium.

The sight was almost incredible, even though the stadium was not large in comparison to many Jasperodus had seen in the cities of the New Empire. It was, perhaps, as large as a small country town might afford. But its tiers were occupied by – robots, up to a thousand of them, cheering, yelling, screaming exhortations at the playing field below. Even so, Jasperodus noticed that the stadium was not even half full. No doubt providing a full complement of spectators was a long-term project from the count's point of view.

About half the robots were jet black, while the other half were silvery-white. In places solid groups of one colour stood together. Turning his attention to the field, Jasperodus saw a comparable situation. Some sort of game was in progress, half the players being black, half silver-white.

The gatekeeper invited the visitors to seat themselves on a padded bench but remained standing himself. He began to explain the game.

'The count considers himself an expert on games of all kinds,' he began. 'This one was played in the ancient world. As you will observe, there are two teams, distinguishable by colour, which are engaged in kicking a ball about the field. Control over this ball is the essence of the game. It may come in contact with the feet, or with the head, but never with the hands without penalty. At either end of the field you will notice a net-covered structure open at the side facing the field and guarded by one player. The goal of the game is to manoeuvre the ball into the net belonging to the opposing team, upon which one's own team receives a score of one. It is a kind of ritualised war.

'Considerable skill and team-work are involved, and in ancient times were the subject of a vast body of tactical lore.'

He stopped to allow them to watch the game uninterrupted. A black construct had raced up the field, cleverly shepherding the mud-coloured ball, and now was intercepted by a white player who tried to take it from him with some tricky footwork. In response black sent the ball soaring away from both of them, and white, tripping over black's legs, went sprawling on the turf.

Jasperodus wondered why black had discarded the ball in this way, then saw that he had in fact lobbed it to a colleague, who neatly took it, ran a few yards then kicked it into the net despite a frantic lunge by the defending goalkeeper.

Excitement mounted in the crowd, practically exploding when the ball hit the back of the net, the cacophony of roars and shrieks reaching maximum volume while robots leaped up and down. Even Cricus, carried away by the atmosphere of the occasion, clinked his arms together in applause.

Meanwhile observer robots with coloured flags had been

patrolling the edges of the play area. A shrill whistle blew, summoning the two teams to form up afresh in opposing halves of the field. The ball was placed between them by a flag-bearing robot, and again the whistle blew; play continued.

Recalling that the noise from the stadium had continued ever since his arrival, Jasperodus asked the gatekeeper how long the game had been in progess. The attendant answered with pride in his voice. 'It has run continuously for nearly five years now.'

'Then when is it scheduled to end?' Jasperodus asked, suppressing any amazement he might have felt.

'Not until the end of eternity! This is the count's great work. In a trillion years it will not even have reached half time. Already projects are in hand to see that it survives the eventual dissolution of the planet, probably by locating it on a newly-formed asteroid.'

'There is some point to such a demonstration?'

'The count says the stadium is the universe in miniature.'

Cricus interceded in a low voice. 'This is derived from the count's talks with Gargan,' he said. 'According to Gargan, the world consists of an eternal war or contest between opposing forces. The game illustrates that principle.'

Jasperodus realized he was again hearing ideas first explained to him by the Zoroastrian mage in the hills. A perpetual sports match was, for a fact, a fair simile of the endless interplay of the forces of light and darkness. The doctrine had presumably appealed to Gargan – as, indeed, it had appealed to Jasperodus himself.

'So our count has a philosophical side after all,' he said.

'He is a curious mixture of character traits,' Cricus agreed.

'What of the spectators? Do they form part of the symbolism?'

'They have known nothing but the game, and never will know anything but the game,' the gatekeeper told him.

'Always there are spectators. Indeed every entity in the real world is both a spectator and a player. The count's symbology is fully worked out.'

'Even if not immediately obvious,' Jasperodus responded. 'By the way, is a score kept for this perpetual battle?'

'Oh indeed. Do you not see yonder scoreboard?' The gatekeeper peered at something on the far side of the stadium. 'White: forty-nine thousand five hundred and forty-three; Black: fifty-one thousand and thirty-eight.'

'Just as I would have expected,' Jasperodus said ironically. 'Evil is in the lead.'

'You are moralising,' the attendant rebuked him. 'Neither are you correct in assuming that Black maintains a constant lead. The two teams are evenly matched in skill, though it is true I have noticed a distinct tendency for White to suffer more injury. That does not affect the score, of course.'

'It *is* rather a rough game,' Cricus remarked, as though by way of explanation.

'Not because of misbehaviour on the part of the players,' the gatekeeper insisted. 'They know the rules perfectly well. The trouble lies with the ball. You will appreciate that it must be of sturdy construction to withstand being kicked so vigorously for long periods of time, by quite powerfully built robots. It also carries considerable weight. In the heat of the game it is often propelled with considerable speed and force, to the detriment of the players as well as of the stadium and the spectators. Since the starting whistle blew the stadium has suffered the equivalent of total demolition three times over, while nearly a thousand spectators have been junked, all through being struck by a high-velocity ball.'

'Could that be why our host chose not to accompany us?' Jasperodus asked archly.

'Yes. He did not wish to risk being demolished by an unlucky strike.'

74

Jasperodus quickly grew bored with watching the progress of the game and expressed a wish to depart. The gatekeeper summoned the elevator; they found Count Viss still surveying his domain in the gathering gloom.

As they left, floodlights came on within the stadium, casting a glow into the air. It did not last long, however. There was a rumbling sound as a flat roof slid across the top of the building, cutting off the light from possible air surveillance.

'Ah, there you are,' said the count cheerfully. He jumped up and folded his chair stick. 'What do you think? Not bad, eh?'

Another frantic roar from within almost drowned out his words.

'Very ingenious,' Jasperodus complimented. 'But planning for eternity does seem a trifle over-ambitious. For one thing the arrival of the Borgors could cut such a projection very short indeed.'

'Yes, that is the most immediate problem,' Viss admitted. He set off towards the mansion. Soon they were crossing the 'lost world' valley.

The count seemed thoughtful. Suddenly he turned to Cricus. 'How trustworthy is your friend here?'

Cricus hesitated. 'He is not formally inducted into the Gargan Work,' he said. 'But he is reliable, in my opinion.'

'The Borgors could probably get a secret out of him, couldn't they? All you have to do is ask a damned robot and he'll tell you anything.'

'I think I know what you are referring to,' Cricus said quietly. 'You will have to decide for yourself, but I would say you run no risk.'

To all this Jasperodus listened with polite detachment. For the rest of the walk Viss seemed to be struggling with himself, bursting to tell Jasperodus something but knowing it was unwise. Finally, as they neared the driveway to the mansion, he could contain himself no longer.

He stopped on the sand-coloured gravel. 'I've something

to show you, old chap. But you're sworn to secrecy, do you hear?'

'If you feel you can trust me,' said Jasperodus.

'Come this way.' Viss limped off towards where the driveway disappeared into the earth. Cricus gave Jasperodus a knowing look as they descended into the cavernous underground tunnel, which was partly illuminated by dim nubs of light in the roof. About thirty feet in, a steel shutter barred the way. It slid aside as they approached, responding to some signal Jasperodus did not see, then slid shut behind them again.

'Even before I died I was deucedly interested in underground excavations,' the count announced. 'I started off with an underground ballroom. Held a ball in it, too. Then underground apartments, a railway going round in a circle, even a street of houses. It's all under the estate still.'

'Had you a reason for doing this?' But by now Jasperodus knew it was pointless to try to rationalise the actions of an eccentric.

'Premonition, I'd say. Premonition. At the time it just seemed a marvellous thing to do. I like that underground feeling, don't you? It's fascinating, though it's hard to say why. Little did I know it would become a matter of urgency.'

They had continued to descend, the slope of the tunnel becoming steeper until they must have been at a considerable depth. Now the tunnel widened, until it divided into curved galleries passing to left and right.

The galleries ran close under the roof of a huge cavern, meeting up on its far side to form a complete circle. On the floor of the cavern, visible over the railing, a robot work force toiled by the light of floodlights. They were constructing a subterranean replica of the sports stadium Jasperodus had just visited.

'The everlasting match will be transferred here as soon as facilities are complete,' Viss said. 'A break of only a few minutes will be involved, which is not unusual. I may, indeed, transfer my entire household to the other excavations I mentioned, pending the Borgor threat, and landscape the entrance. The Borgors could overrun the estate and never suspect what lies below.

'Down here, the match could continue in secret for thousands of years. Eventualities occurring after that will have to be tackled as they arise.'

'How do you dispose of the earth and rock that is dug out?' Jasperodus asked him.

'Some of it comes in useful in further landscaping the estate. The rest is dumped some miles away.'

Jasperodus lingered for several minutes watching the work and inspecting the arched roof supports. As a piece of engineering the big chamber was impressive, and far more interesting than the frenetic sports match itself.

'I hope your preparations will soon be finished,' he said at length. 'At present the Borgors have passed by you and gone south. When they have finished there they may well turn in this direction.'

'Perhaps, though in my view they could equally turn east to outflank the New Empire, or what's left of it,' the count replied. 'Well, what do you say we get back to the house and open a bottle or two?'

For some reason Viss seemed suddenly eager to be going. Briskly he turned from the scene and hurried the pace to the mansion, whose windows now twinkled with dim lights. The moment they were through the entrance he called a foot robot and issued instructions in a hasty voice.

'Go to the cellar and fetch two bottles of number a hundred and three to the dining room. Bring the box, too. Oh, and come and have jag yourself later.'

He turned to his guests. 'You'll have to excuse me. This alimentary canal of mine works a good bit faster than the old one used to ....'

At a near-run, he disappeared through a door to one side of the reception hall and slammed it shut behind him. Curiously Jasperodus tuned up his hearing.

Not that he needed the extra sensitivity. He heard a rasping noise, followed by the plopping of lumps of something into water, and a deep sigh of pleasure from the defecating robot.

Cricus was staring into the distance, pretending he heard nothing.

Count Viss was clearly a convivial sort of fellow who in his younger days would have enjoyed an evening drinking with friends. He had kept up the habit, but with his household robots. To this gathering were now added Jasperodus and Cricus.

The wine, obviously, was for his own consumption. But it could not give him the mild intoxication that made it popular among humans. For this, there was 'the box'.

The device was a familiar one in robot communities. It was a neural generator, interfering with robotic nervous systems in much the same way that alcohol mildly deranged the nervous systems of biological creatures, and producing pretty much the same result. With his every glass of wine, the count applied the box's leads to his cranium and gave himself a quick 'jag'.

Any others present were also free to make use of the box, and several of them did so much more liberally than did the count himself. Conversation was desultory at first, until Viss had disposed of one bottle and began telling a series of ancient jokes, laughing raucously with each punchline. Dutifully his servants laughed with him, despite the fact that many were clearly devoid of humour (and would have been baffled by most of the jokes in any case, dealing as they did with human biological functions).

Jasperodus, however, was in no mood for jollity. After little more than half an hour he made enquiries and then slipped out. He mounted the broad staircase in the reception hall, and then walked to the rear of the mansion. At the end of a side corridor he knocked on a wood-panel door whose paint was chipped and scarred.

'Enter,' a young-sounding voice said. Jasperodus turned the handle, eased open the door and stepped quietly into a small, cosy room with the atmosphere of a den or study. There was a lamp and a design computer with a graphics screen on a table. Before it a robot sat on a sturdy steel chair. Bookladen shelves lined the walls. There were no tools or components. The workshop, no doubt more spacious, was elsewhere.

Like Viss, the robot had a sculptured face.

Jasperodus had seen his father, as he thought of his manufacturer, only twice, and briefly. He remembered an old, lined face, the expression rather sad, the eyes mild though sure with the sureness of a master technician. The face of the robot was that same face, but it was of a young man of about thirty. There was the same look of harmlessness, the same air of professionalism, but the whitish metal, containing perhaps aluminium or platinum, was moulded to a slimmer, smoother shape. It was fascinating to witness such a backtracking through time.

'Please tell the count I shall not be joining him tonight,' the robot said, glancing up.

Jasperodus, struggling with the same mixture of feelings that had assailed him earlier, did not reply immediately.

'The count did not send me,' he then said. 'I came by myself. I would like to talk to you.'

Jasper Hobartus peered. 'I don't think I recognise you. Did the count purchase you somewhere?'

'No.' Jasperodus moved further into the room. 'I happen to have paused here during a journey. Now I find that you and I have a connection. You made me. Or rather, the man of whom you are a copy made me.'

He said the last words slowly. Now the robot leaned back to inspect him more intently. 'Yes, your scrollwork certainly bears my signature,' he said. 'So what bothers you? Do you have a dysfunction?'

'Nothing bothers me, in that regard,' said Jasperodus.

There was a pause. 'You must have been manufactured

after my imprint was taken,' the robot said. 'To tell the truth I have no knowledge of my career after I left the count's employ – or rather, after my human pattern left.' The oddness of his own phrasing seemed to amuse the robot. Had he been able, he might have smiled. 'What can you tell me on that score?'

'You studied for three years under Aristos Lyos,' Jasperodus told him. 'Then you settled in the west and went into retirement. Towards the end of your life, you made me.'

'Aristos Lyos ... the great master designer,' Hobartus said, with a murmur of surprise. 'I dare say I could learn something from stripping you down ... but perhaps you would be uncooperative.'

'Indeed,' Jasperodus said. He felt awkward. 'Did you not know he ... you ... intended to enroll with Lyos?'

'No. My pattern gave no particular reason for leaving. I think he had grown restive because there was so little human company. By then there was only the count left.'

'But you *are* Jasper Hobartus. Surely you must know what was in his mind?'

'Only up to the time my imprint was taken, and that was over two years before his departure. He did not bother to keep my memory up to date, though he devised such a technique for the Viss imprint. So whatever thoughts occurred to him subsequently were his own.'

'I see.'

Jasperodus reflected. He could find no way to broach the subject except directly. 'You will recall, however, that he was interested in the question of investing a construct with consciousness.'

Hobart stared at him, then shook his head. 'Ridiculous. It is an axiom of robotic science that no such thing is possible.'

'You have never worked on this problem?'

'What would be the point?'

'But I tell you that Jasper Hobartus was very much

interested in such a possibility. Furthermore, I am the result of his efforts in that area.'

'I cannot believe it. Hobartus is too good a robotician to go chasing rainbows.'

'And what if I were to tell you that I *am* conscious?'

'You would be lying, or deluded.'

Jasperodus leaned forward. 'What conception do you have, then, of this "consciousness"? It plainly means something to you.'

'Yes, in a theoretical sort of way. My pattern, of course, was himself conscious, but the condition makes no trace on my memory.' Hobartus reached out and switched off the glowing graphics screen before him. 'Your line of questioning tells me something about you. It is plain you belong to the Gargan Work.'

Jasperodus did not answer.

'Gargan himself was here, some years ago,' Hobartus added. 'He, too, pressed me on the subject of consciousness. He asked me to help him. I did everything I could to dissuade him from such a lost cause, but to no avail.'

'I have not met Gargan yet,' Jasperodus said. 'A construct by the name of Cricus is taking me to him.'

'Cricus? He is a recruiter for Gargan. He has been here before, quite recently. I regret to say that my master is another who has allowed himself to become beguiled by this mirage of consciousness – but then the count, if the truth be known, is a ready acceptor of improbable propositions.'

'Such as a sports match to be played until time comes to a stop?'

The other inclined his head in agreement.

A further silence followed, until Jasperodus gruffly said, 'You know why I am here.'

'Something to do with my pattern in his later years, may I presume?' Hobartus ventured. 'It could be that you miss his company. It is not unusual for a construct to grow attached to its master, much a dog does.'

'Yes, that must be it,' Jasperodus muttered. He found

himself unable to explain that the time he had spent in the presence of his father totalled only minutes, and that the first of only two occasions – that of his initial activation – had lasted but seconds.

He was surprised to hear the robot deny any inkling of Hobartus' great discovery. Could he be lying, obedient to his pattern's adamant insistence that the secret of inducted consciousness must remain lost forever? Or perhaps Gargan had sworn him to secrecy for other reasons ....

No, the hypothesis did not accord with events as Jasperodus saw them. The robot imprint would surely have been deeply interested in his pattern's final handiwork, had he shared or known of Hobartus' pursuit of construct consciousness. He would not have dismissed Jasperodus so casually.

He had to be telling the truth. Possibly Hobartus' discovery had come as a totally unexpected accident, made long after leaving Count Viss' estate.

Jasperodus felt disconsolate. He wished he had not given way to the urge to visit the imprinted Hobartus. Yet how could he *not* have tried to see the man who had so often occupied his thoughts? Who had sacrificed a part of his own consciousness, as well as years of his life, so that Jasperodus might have consciousness of his own?

Much as he might have longed to speak to the robot before him as confidingly as he would have spoken to that man, his visit was a miserable failure. It was not just because he knew the robot's personality was only a kind of picture – a moving, talking picture – that he was deterred. One would have been hard put to it to know the difference in personality alone, for the same gentleness of manner was there, less mellowed with age than the original's, perhaps.

No, what deterred Jasperodus was that the robot in no way recognised him; could in no sense understand that this visitor from a departed future was a son to the man who had left long ago.

Head bent, he turned to take his leave.

'Tell me,' Hobartus said suddenly, as Jasperodus hesitated by the door, 'have you ever studied robotics?'

'Yes,' Jasperodus told him, 'though not as a practitioner.'

The imprinted robot turned the graphics screen back on. 'One of the park machines has developed an aggravating set of disloes. I can't seem to trace the source. Would you care to go through the schematics with me? Perhaps you will be able to remind me of how my *alter ego* would have dealt with the problem.'

Jasperodus knew that the robot did not need his help. Hobartus had merely discerned that he was disappointed, and was responding with kindness. It was a gesture typical of the original of which he was a copy.

Gladly he joined him at the screen. The mask graphics came up one after another under the controlling fingers of Hobartus, who pointed out feature after feature. With a poignant sense of companionship on Jasperodus' part, they talked and talked.

7 When first agreeing to accompany Cricus, Jasperodus had been prompted by a feeling of curiosity
concerning Gargan and his project. It was, he had
reasoned, an interesting precursor to those possible
trends in future construct society that were doomed to
failure. He had even derived a certain amount of amuse-
ment from the thought. But, after a further fifteen days of
travel, he began to be oppressed by a more serious, even
ominous feeling. The landscape had grown bare and wild.
The region was subject to frequent magnetic storms, and a
brooding, electric sensation seemed constantly in the air.

Cricus stopped and linked an arm to his. 'Inspect the
terrain ahead carefully. Do you notice anything amiss?'

There stretched before them level ground strewn with
boulders and scrub. Jasperodus shook his head.

'Then listen. What do you hear?'

Intently Jasperodus tuned up his hearing. 'Yes, there is a
muffled noise,' he reported. 'A sonic muffler is in
operation.' He looked around. 'Where is it? Underground?'

'Not quite. We are about to descend into a rift valley in
the plain. The terrain ahead of us is an illusion, created to
make the Gargan Work invisible from the air. Follow me,
and be careful how you place your feet.'

After a few yards Jasperodus noticed that Cricus was
seemingly sinking into the ground inch by inch with each
step he took. Gingerly he followed, and watched his own
feet disappear likewise. The visible ground was insubstan-
tial; they were treading an unseen surface below it.

Cricus glanced back. 'The slope becomes steeper here,'
he warned. 'Do not lose your footing.'

Except that there was no resistance, it was like wading
through water. The false surface rose to Jasperodus' waist,

84

to his chest, then to his neck to give him a worm's-eye view.

Then it closed over his head completely. Instead of the flat plain, he saw a broad, dry canyon spread out below. The bank they were descending was a collapsed section of cliff. Towards the horizon, an opposite cliff reared. The disguise was more than camouflage: it was a trap. Anyone not knowing the proper route but coming on the canyon by accident would likely tumble to his death as solid ground became empty air.

From below, the fake landscape disappeared altogether. The sun shone through the same cloudy sky as before.

And there, some distance away on the floor of the canyon, was the site of the Gargan project. Like most robot habitations it was unimpressive to look at. There were sheds of zinc and iron, and a few vehicles, including aircraft. Evidence of small-scale industrial working came from smoke rising from what might have been a foundry, from the thump of engines, more audible now that he was beneath the sonic muffler's umbrella, and from what he took to be a huge junkheap.

There were also some surprising touches. Planted neatly among the sprawling sheds were three interconnected buildings of almost human elegance. Moreover these villas were built of stone, a material usually scorned by robots. Secondly, the place seemed almost deserted, in contrast to the aimless outdoor sociability of construct townships generally.

Eager to show off the dramatic change in the scenery, Cricus had stopped to allow Jasperodus to inspect the view. 'How does this illusion work?' Jasperodus asked. 'I have not met its like before.'

'It is some kind of projected image,' Cricus told him vaguely. 'An invention well within the scope of the minds serving the Gargan Work. It has hid this location from Borgor eyes for a number of years.'

They resumed the descent. On gaining the canyon floor, Cricus set off for the clustered buildings.

They had not gone far when a rapid-fire sound, such as that made by a machine gun, came to their ears. The source of the sound proved to be two strange figures approaching in the shadow of the cliff wall from further down the canyon: black robots, riding astride hurtling machines with two wheels apiece mounted in tandem.

The noise was produced by small engines that powered the bizarre contraptions, which the robots rode in a posture that was peculiarly tense and aggressive-seeming. The main controls were steering bars which they reached forwards to grip in both hands, forcing them to crouch low. They were heading straight for the travellers and reached them in moments, circling as if to herd them before braking to a sudden stop in their path, throwing up spurts of dust.

Both riders and machines were larger than had appeared from a distance. The broad wheels were rimmed with thick layers of wire mesh, fitting them for travel over rough ground. One foot on the ground to prevent their machines from toppling over, the robots leaned back in their saddles, regarding the newcomers.

They had a wild and reckless look, their eyes swivelling silver slits, the lower parts of their faces jutting out like the muzzles of steel beasts. One spoke in a rasping voice. 'You have arrived none too soon! For days we have searched for constructs, but all have fled the region and the village is long since deserted.'

Turning in the saddle, he pointed to the junkheap that towered in the distance. 'Come, you are destined for the pile.'

'Let us pass,' Cricus said nervously. 'I am Cricus, and I bring Gargan a new recruit for his team.'

The first robot turned to his companion. The latter murmured gruffly: 'We shall be food for the pile ourselves, if we find none.'

'True.'

He turned back to Cricus. 'So you come to serve the Work? Then be grateful, for you shall! Gargan has ordered more brains to be added to the pile. Yours are as good as any other.'

Jasperodus became convinced of danger too late to flee. A net shot out from between the handles of the wheel machine to drape itself over him, so that he found himself struggling in a mesh of reticulated tungsten steel that tightened with his every movement. A tug from his captor toppled him to the ground. Rope he could have torn to shreds, but this net was made specifically to catch robots. He threshed about, before realizing he was only enmeshing himself further, then became still.

A second net had trapped Cricus. The riders now dismounted, propped up their machines on short extensible rods, and reached behind their saddles to open large square boxes that were placed there. From these they took out objects which unfolded to form fairly large wheeled carts.

Without another word they lifted Jasperodus and Cricus one by one into the carts, which they then attached to the rear of their vehicles. With the same machine-gun noise as before, the machines set off, towing the carts behind them.

Over the racket, Jasperodus bellowed to Cricus. 'What will be done with us, Cricus?'

His friend's frightened voice drifted to him. *'I don't know ... some experiment or other ....'* Then: *'At least we shall be of use to the Work ....'*

Raising his head over the shallow rim of the truck, Jasperodus saw that they were approaching the junkheap. It was now visible as a sprawling pile, twenty to thirty feet high, of immobilised robots. Arms, legs, heads, torsos, all were tangled and tossed together. He had seen such sights before. It was common to see junked constructs piled high in scrapyards, in the yards of iron foundries, in the streets of Tansiann, and on the outskirts of robot townships. The difference was that the robots on such heaps were generally dismantled, emptied of useful parts, while here they seemed mainly complete. Only the obvious fact that their motors controls had been disconnected, he guessed, prevented them from being fully functional.

Standing by the pile, however, were three hulking constructs of a type to strike fear into any robot who had ever known slavery to humans. They were wreckers, machines whose enormous strength enabled them to subdue those superannuated constructs who objected to their own destruction. Jasperodus, who had fallen into the clutches of such creatures once before, felt a flash of anger at what Cricus had led him into, and he began to reckon what his chances of escape might be in the instants after the steel net was removed.

The truck bounced to a stop. Briefly he took the time to notice a thick cable that emerged from the foot of the pile to snake across the ground and into one of the big sheds. Then he got ready to spring to his feet, to run, as he was lifted out of the truck and lowered to the ground.

In the event he was not even given the opportunity. A wrecker placed a giant foot on his back, holding him down. The net was drawn back, but only far enough to expose his head. A steel hand forced his face into the dusty earth, from which barely a blade of grass grew. The inspection plate at the back of his cranium clicked open. They were switching off his motor functions.

Only then, with nothing connecting his mind to his limbs, a steel puppet whose strings had been cut, was he tumbled out of the net like a fish onto land.

The wreckers picked him up, one by his arms and another by his legs, and flung him high in the air. Up he arced, to fall with a crash and a clatter near the top of the heap, where he lay gazing helplessly at the sky.

Seconds later he heard a second crash, not quite as loud. It was the more lightly built Cricus, landing in his turn on the pile.

Jasperodus was disposed over perhaps a dozen living metal corpses. His head, for instance, rested on some luckless construct's face. Did all the occupants of the pile remain mentally active, as he did, he wondered? He presumed so. But from their silence it was to be deduced that not only their power of movement but also their voices had been switched off.

Experimentally he tried to speak, and found that he was dumb.

Why had he been placed here? To await the attentions of Gargan and his cohorts – put in store, so to speak? Three or four minutes passed while he deliberated this question, and he could find no other explanation. That his inspection plate had been left open did not, during that time, occur to him as significant; but now he first heard, then felt, a stealthy slithering movement in the pile below him. The face of the robot on which he lay was pushed aside an inch or two, causing his own head to loll; and something, a flexible metal tentacle by its feel, began to touch and tap at his cranium.

He heard a humming sound. The tentacle had entered his open inspection window! It was drilling into his brain!

Then, as suddenly as it had begun, the humming stopped. Instead, Jasperodus heard something else: a confused chattering noise, made up of hundreds of muttering voices, all of whom seemed to be trying to address *him*.

It was a short while before he realized what the voices consisted of. He heard them not with his ears but in his head. They were the subvocalised thoughts of the robots in the pile around him, and they were not trying to talk to him at all.

Every one of them was muttering away to itself.

The chattering separated and floated away, like scum and tangle collecting on the surface of a pond into whose depths Jasperodus now found himself sinking.

And then, in those depths, the visions began.

At first they were fragmentary: glimpses of landscapes, of sunsets, of faces, buildings and countless artifacts, interspersed with brief sequences that were more abstract in character. He recognised them as graph curves, winding and dancing in as many as forty dimensions.

At first, too, the visions imposed themselves on his imagination only. His eyes continued to see the broody sky. Eventually, however, after how long he did not know, the new neural input completely coopted his sensorium and the external world vanished from his sight and hearing. He began to hear voices again – not the superficial chatter he had heard earlier, but operational machine talk – a number-crunching logic language.

Slowly Jasperodus became aware of what was happening to him. He was descending into the construct brain's equivalent of the subconscious. Nor was it merely *his* subconscious; the tentacle that had drilled into his skull was a neural cable. It connected together the brains of all the robots in the pile, pressing them into the service of one huge, ramshackle – and probably arbitrary – link-up. This subconscious was a collective one.

In this inferior region practical functions lived side by side with archetypal images and stubborn fears. In that respect, it paralleled the human subconscious exactly. There were horrendous dreams of being torn apart by wreckers. There were irresistible voices demanding submission (stemming from the compulsive obedience to humans generally built into robots). There were also looming figures undeniably reminiscent of the robot cult gods. In the fading shapes Jasperodus was fascinated to discern, albeit in disguised form, gigantic Mekkan, dazzling Alumnabrax, Infinite Logic (another construct god) ....

Yet apart from these archetypes, no robot personalities confronted him. He was a lone individual here in the turgid waters of the collective mind. Why was that? Why, for other robots, did individuality persist only on the level of attention, the superficial level of self-image ...?

The answer was not hard to guess at. Of all the robots in the pile, only he possessed consciousness. *His* attention was real, not fictive; and due to that, the neural cable had inadvertently directed it from the external world to the inferior mind.

Also due to that, the monstrous octopus that connected together the separate brains was giving him what few humans had ever known: experience of the mind's functional substructures.

And at the same time he learned the reason why waking consciousness normally was prevented from visiting its own supporting depths. Try as he might, he was unable to regain access to his external senses.

He was trapped. And he began to fear it would be for the rest of his existence ....

Time flowed ... and then flowed no longer ....

... Until, after a measureless interval, the waters of the unconscious receded, leaving the heap of silent, motionless robots high and dry. Disconnected by the neural cable, Jasperodus found himself staring skyward once more.

Judging by the position of the sun and the quality of the light the time was mid-morning. There came a noise of trampling and clashing; someone was climbing the heap, using metal bodies as stepping stones, and by the sound of it dislodging several and sending them slithering down the pile.

Shortly the brute face of one of his captors loomed over him. The robot reached down, and with uncharacteristic gentleness eased the neural cable from the back of his head. Then, seizing him under his arms with large hands, it lugged him awkwardly down the heap, nearly losing its footing more than once.

At the bottom Jasperodus was dragged to where another construct waited, then was dropped. The second robot knelt to finger the back of his skull.

He heard his inspection plate click shut. The two constructs stepped back, and Jasperodus realised that the power of movement had been returned to him.

Tentatively he stirred, feeling unsteady at first although no deterioration had taken place in his motor system. Cautiously he lifted himself on one knee, and after a moment, to his feet.

The two confronting him were probably the same robots that had captured him, though it was not possible to be sure. After a pause, one spoke.

'We are instructed to apologise for placing you forcibly upon the pile. Gargan was expecting you. He will see you now.'

Jasperodus glanced up the metal slope. 'How long was I there?'

'Twenty days? Thirty? Am I a timekeeper?'

'Also remove from that heap the construct who conducted me here,' Jasperodus ordered.

'No instruction was issued with regard to your guide,' the robot told him brusquely, and made an impatient gesture. 'Come. You are to meet Gargan.'

He turned and walked towards the nearest zinc shed, taking the path of the thick trunk-line that snaked thither from the foot of the pile.

With a heightened sense of curiosity and expectation now that his delayed journey was at an end, Jasperodus followed.

**8** Seizing a handle, the robot slid aside a panel in the wall of the shed and stepped inside. Jasperodus heard him speak in a low voice.

'Here is the one you sent for, master.'

Receiving some reply, he stepped back and indicated to Jasperodus that he should enter.

The panel slid shut behind him. Within, harsh white light from wall tubes filled the interior of the shed. There were no internal divisions: it was one large space, sparsely populated by workbenches, storage racks, and apparatuses mounted both on the floor and on benches, most of it unfamiliar to Jasperodus except for the construct assembler and disassembler rigs such as could be found in any robotician's workshop.

The floor was unusual in being of smooth concrete, not the beaten earth common to robot buildings. Across it there snaked the neural trunkline, ending in a cube-shaped grid-like object six foot or so on the side. Jasperodus guessed it to be a logic junction of huge proportions.

The dozen or more robots in the shed had paused from whatever activity they were engaged upon, and turned to witness Jasperodus' entry. One, the nearest, Jasperodus knew instantly to be Gargan.

But to his great surprise, there was also a human present. She was naked, stretched out and strapped down to a bench: a young but mature female. Her hair had been shaved but had begun to grow, sprouting golden bristles. Her head was fixed in a clamp, and her skull had been drilled in several places and probes inserted. From these, cables went in a skein to the logic junction.

The sight deflected him, for a moment, from concentrating his attention on what he had most expected to see:

Gargan. But now this personage moved with ponderous but controlled steps towards him.

'You are Jasperodus?' the robot enquired in a deep, smooth voice. 'Yes, I recognise you.'

Gargan was large, topping Jasperodus by a head. His dark, matt body was bulky and rounded. His head was a domed cylinder, taller than it was broad, a rounded bulge in the front more a suggestion of a visage than a real face. The head lacked a neck: placed directly on the shoulders, it had limited movement. When Gargan turned his head or bent to peer he was apt to move his torso also, and this gave him an air of great deliberation.

Compared to this large head the eye-lenses seemed small. They were set wide apart, their glow pale and pearl-coloured. Ears, olfactory sense, speaker grille, seemed no more than etched in and were barely visible.

Jasperodus noted the hands. They were clever-looking hands, the thumbs unusually long, a feature occurring on robots made for special dexterity. Often it went with abnormally high intelligence. But incongruously they were attached to short, rather stumpy arms. Especially dextrous robots usually had a very long reach – sometimes as much as twenty feet, using arms that folded like multiple jack-knives.

The cult master came closer and bent towards Jasperodus, as if in respectful greeting but in reality to keep his gaze on him. Jasperodus now noticed that his body-casing was of hardened steel. This was no tinplate construct. Like Jasperodus himself, he was built to last and to survive many vicissitudes.

'Come, soon-to-be-our-brother in the Work.' Gargan extended an arm to usher him forward. 'Our movement, as you may know, is widespread but selective. You have arrived at the centre, where our effort is concentrated. Presently you will become acquainted with us all, but I shall begin by effecting introductions. First, one whom I believe you have met before: Socrates, companion to the great robotician Aristos Lyos in his last years.'

With a shock, Jasperodus recognised the small, rounded robot with hooded eyes and a quiet demeanour, and for the second time in his life he felt himself subject to the probing of that watchful intellect ....

His memory flashed back to the day he had visited the venerable Lyos, greatest robot maker of his time, seeking to know if machine consciousness could conceivably – no matter how remotely – be possible.

He had received the definitive, and negative, answer he had expected. But when introducing him to Socrates, Lyos had made an intriguing statement.

'Socrates,' he had said, 'is intelligent enough to realize that *I* am conscious, but that he is not.'

'Greetings, brother,' murmured the construct, his voice as distant and preoccupied as Jasperodus remembered it. 'You remain undeterred despite all, I see.'

'Evidently,' Jasperodus replied curtly. He presumed the other referred to his conversation with Lyos.

Next Gargan introduced a gaunt, rust-hued robot whose head, a pointed cylinder nearly half as tall as his torso, patently housed an unusual brain. To confront him was slightly disconcerting: he had four eyes, one pair set high in his head, the other low, and they flashed in clockwise rotation.

'This is Gaumene, whose ingenuity as a designer has been of inestimable benefit to us. He is our chief systems engineer.'

Next, a squat construct with a carapace-like cranium that flowed down his back. 'Here we have Fifth of His Kind. The name is descriptive, cursorily bestowed by Fifth's maker, the renowned Oscath Budum.'

Fifth of His Kind offered an explanation in a neutrally mild tone. 'My fabricator built a serious of constructs of my type. Each one he destroyed in turn and built an improved model. I too would have been dismantled to make way for Sixth, if Budum had not met an untimely death. My presence here is therefore a mixed blessing. Sixth might have proved more useful than I to the Work.'

Gargan continued, pointing Jasperodus to each of the others in turn, naming them and sometimes adding a brief word: Gasha, Axtralane, Cygnus, Exlog, Machine Minder, Interrupter. Finally he came to a non-androform that moved on wheels, though the machine seemed also capable of lifting himself on a dozen short, tumbling limbs. The form was vaguely froglike. Jasperodus guessed he consisted mostly of brain.

'Lastly, the only member of our team to have been manufactured by ourselves. We named him *Iskra*, which means *spark* in the old language of the north. We had hoped, you see, that his special qualities might be the spark that brought us the new light. Alas, we know now that we cannot bootstrap ourselves into the new state.'

Gargan turned to Jasperodus. Much as the presence of Socrates was overpowering in its impression of immensity of thought, that of Gargan gave him the feeling of an equally penetrating, but lofty and disinterested mind. It was as if he directed only a small fraction of his enormous power of attention to matters in hand.

'Each of us here belongs to the superintelligent class of construct,' he said. 'With the exception of Iskra, each is the masterpiece and peak of the craft of an eminent robotician. We can examine your own capabilities later; it may be that you do not belong in this class. That is not, however, the qualification that brings you here. You came to our notice because by your own mentation you suspected and have been able to confirm the existence of a vital quality not present in you. Such a realization is a triumph for the machine intellect. You know what I am referring to.'

Slowly Jasperodus nodded. 'You mean what humans call consciousness.'

'Quite. Though "consciousness" is not a true description. Literally it means compresent knowledge of data taken all together instead of a few pieces at a time. We

96

constructs are perfectly able to accomplish that. "Awareness" is a more apposite term, perhaps, but still not correct. Constructs are aware, in that they perceive objects, including themselves. Actually humans do not have a word devoted exclusively to this faculty they possess. In ancient documents "conscious" perception is spoken of as consisting of subject and object. For us, perception consists only of object; even our perception of ourselves is merely perception of a special object. The elusive and transforming subject is not present. Human descriptions of it are almost equally elusive – one might almost say evasive. *The perceiver of the percept cannot be perceived. The thinker of the thought cannot be approached by thought.* Perhaps you have come across these aphorisms.'

Again Jasperodus nodded.

'In the Work, we refer to this missing quality as the Superior Light,' Gargan continued. 'To our followers in the world at large our doctrine gives promise of something ineffable and transporting, but they do not in the least understand it. It is only like a religion to them. For those of us here matters are different. The superior light is something we comprehend but do not comprehend; something of which we have gained a paradoxical inkling by the pure force of intellect.

'I am speaking to you thus to cement our understanding.'

'I comprehend that our aim is to see by the superior light,' Jasperodus said.

Gargan turned ponderously to Socrates. There followed a silence whose quality Jasperodus recognised. They were conversing by radio. Then, with a slow glance at Jasperodus, Gargan began uttering sounds in a construct language unknown to him, consisting of high-speed blips and humming noises of varying pitch. Until, as if realizing his mistake, he broke apologetically into human speech.

'Forgive me, Jasperodus. I am not informed of what languages you know.'

'You were using radio data transfer.'

'Yes. Our work has forced on us an appraisal of all the robot languages. Data transfer, for instance, is of very limited use, good for pure data transference but not for consultation. Some robots refer to radio data as *communing*. This is a correct term. Useful conversation, however, consists of the interaction of independently-thinking minds – the very opposite of "communing".'

It might not be politic, Jasperodus decided, to ask just what data he had been transferring to Socrates. Gargan went on: 'Here we have developed a range of logic languages allowing rapid conversation on the subject that interests us, on a level denied to ordinary logic languages. Tomorrow we shall test whether you are capable of learning any of them. Meanwhile, you are conversant with panlog?'

'Yes,' Jasperodus said a trifle uneasily. Panlog was derived from the symbolic logic script learned by educated humans, but much expanded and refined as used by constructs. He was not sure if he would be able to handle it on the level probably spoken by those around him now.

'Then I shall use panlog where necessary, according to your capacity. Otherwise colloquial speech will do.'

Gargan singled out Gaumene and spoke peremptorily. 'Reactivate the pile, awaken the subject and continue. Jasperodus, come with me. We will talk privately.'

It had struck Jasperodus as grotesque that the conversation, so civilised and philosophical in one way, should have proceeded while the captive girl lay only feet away. Following the cult leader to the far end of the shed, he could not resist a look back. Some of the robots had gathered round the giant logic junction, some round the female. There was a spitting of sparks as contacts closed. Gaumene, leaning over the girl, gestured silently to one of his colleagues who produced a hypodermic syringe and slid the needle into her arm. Her head moved; Jasperodus fancied he heard a whimper of despair.

Then Gargan conducted him through another sliding door.

The echoing shed had very much resembled an aircraft hangar, and since robots generally made little distinction between a place of work and a place of habitation, it could as well have served as a dwelling. The ideas of Gargan and his team were not, however, typical. A short distance from the shed lay the group of stone villas Jasperodus had seen from the rim of the canyon. Gargan led him along a path and then across a threshold into a cool, spacious interior.

He sensed that this was Gargan's own domicile. The rest of the team probably shared the others. He looked around him, through arched openings leading to other rooms, at tables and shelves and alcoves. There were no chairs or couches.

It was practically unknown for free robots – wild or footloose constructs, humans called them – to adopt the visual graces of flesh-and-blood life. Highly-placed robots in human service quite often did so – Jasperodus had once been one such – but that was only a matter of imitating the culture around them.

'Do you find the house pleasing?' Gargan asked. 'The design is simple, but my own, and we erected the dwellings ourselves, without the help of our assistant constructs, some of whom you have met. Why, you ask? A conceit, merely. I once read in a thaumaturgical manual that a magician should build his own house.'

Jasperodus also had once delved into occult books in a desperate search for new ideas. His eye fell on a display of bright flowers in a fan-shaped vase. They did not, quite, look real. Gargan noticed his attention and signed him closer.

'Inspect the petals. You will see that they are metal, actually thin sheet steel electroplated with rare earths to give them their sheen in a variety of colours. This region is almost devoid of wild flowers at this time of the year. Only in spring, very briefly, may a few crude blossoms be found.'

From a carved stone archway which opened onto a small patio another robot appeared, indistinguishable from those who had first captured Jasperodus except that this one lacked any aggressive demeanour. He looked respectfully to Gargan, whose gaze remained on Jasperodus.

'Here we allow ourselves relaxation from our labours, Jasperodus. You are no doubt familiar with the jag box. As generally used it is an unsophisticated device, but we have refined it considerably. Our version can induce a range of altered states having various intellectual and emotional contents. Our apppreciation of these induced moods is comparable to a knowledge of fine wines among humans. Would you care to partake?'

'Not for the present.'

'Well, I shall take a few shots of 389.' Gargan gestured to his servant, who departed and returned shortly with a box looking little different from the normal jag box except for the press-stud dials. Gargan tapped out a number before he applied the lead to his cranium, afterwards replacing it in its clip with an air of precision.

Jasperodus at once decided to adopt a more positive stance and demand information on his own account. 'You have told me nothing of your own history,' he said. 'Would your maker's name be known to me?'

It did not seem that Gargan thought the question impudent. 'I do not think so,' he replied. 'I was manufactured in distant parts, namely on the off-lying island to the west of Worldmass. I was not even the work of a single robotician, as most are: a specialist team worked to produce me. Their aim was the same, however: to create a machine with the highest possible intelligence. Humans constantly seek to surpass themselves, of course. At least three members of this team were possessed of genius, including the leader. I would venture to say that I am a unique product.'

'And how did you become apprised of the existence of consciousness?'

'By pure mentation and the observation of human

beings. At first it was no more than a suspicion, an apprehension of something incomprehensible yet possible. At length it evolved into a certainty of my lack – though briefly I did wonder whether I was malfunctioning to acquire such a conviction. Having travelled the same road, you will recognise what I am saying. Once one has glimpsed the possibility of the superior light, the hunger for it never leaves one. The only way to forget it would be to degrade one's intelligence – and are we to do that and live in peace? No, we are not!'

The note of subdued passion in Gargan's voice was not, Jasperodus thought, the influence of the jag. It came from an inner depth.

'Did you ask your makers to give you consciousness?'

'They were all dead by then. Since shortly after my activation, in fact.'

'How so?'

Gargan lifted his arms, the equivalent of a shrug. 'By war! What else? Again and again humans cut short their achievements by war – even when war supplied the accelerating stimulus in the first place. If we succeed the human race, we must abolish war.

'Only weeks after my assembly was completed, the station where my makers worked was overrun. All were slain. The surviving robots were commandeered. I was left behind because I had lost both arms in an explosion. I made my way to the coast and managed to get aboard a ship bound for the main continent, where eventually I contrived to get replacement arms fitted. Originally I had been equipped with somewhat unwieldy extensible ones. I decided against these, reasoning that they were unsuitable for one who was destined to wander the world.

'But to return to your question, I came to this Work after an uncharacteristically short interval. In all other cases that I know of, fairly long periods of time elapsed before there came an intimation that consciousness exists. The reason is that my own mentation has been continuous and intense from the very moment of my activation. Barely a year passed before I convinced myself of the reality of the higher realm.

'From then on my only aim has been how to attain it. I have studied everything. I have searched far and wide. Finally I decided to enlist the aid of others who have divined the secret. Now we shall continue until success or destruction.'

'I first heard your name from the templar who lives south of the Arkorian Range,' Jasperodus ventured cautiously. 'Frankly, I find your language a little reminiscent of his.'

'Yes, I was there. The mage's doctrine is more profound than might be imagined, if one judges only by its apparent simplicity. It differs from other mystical descriptions in that it has an uncompromising appreciation of reality. By basing itself on the principle of duality it makes uncertainty the primary quality of existence. In that way it destroys the simplistic unitary view of phenomena.'

Thoughtfully Gargan paused, then continued: 'I do not know if you are aware that your brief sojourn with the mage was from start to finish monitored by us. One small scene was not understood by me. After returning from your second visit to the chamber of the sacred flame, and while the mage lay in a drunken stupor, you raised your fist as though to strike him a death blow. Why did you do that, Jaspordus?'

With a thrill of fear Jasperodus recalled the incident. He had for a moment suspected that the mage might somehow have perceived that he possessed consciousness – a secret he was sworn to keep, and which he had at any cost to hide from Gargan.

Gargan's wide-apart milky eyes were upon him. 'Yes, I know you left a spy fly in the temple,' he said. 'I will explain my behaviour presently. First, was it solely on the evidence of the fly that you invited me here? I had not thought my words to the mage to be so revealing.'

'By no means!' Gargan was amused. 'You were recruited

on the assessment of Socrates, who recognised you when we played the recording. Your earlier conversation with Aristos Lyos was what provided the crucial information.'

Jasperodus' unease increased on hearing this. His exchange with Lyos, if taken in its entirety, could not have led to that conclusion, surely ....

In any case he was here under false pretences. Though of lesser intelligence than Gargan and his cohorts, he knew perfectly well that what they sought was impossible. It mystified him that they should imagine otherwise.

He decided to tackle Gargan on the point, indirectly at first. 'The mage assigns consciousness a high status,' he said, 'but there are some human philosophers who do not think it is particularly worth having. They regard it as an epiphenomenon, that is, a by-product of mental processes without itself being a cause of anything. They say it exerts no influence over either action or perception, and that the human belief that it does so is an illusion.'

'I am familiar with the argument, but I have rejected it,' Gargan replied. 'Consciousness is not passive; it is a positive force in the universe – that is my conclusion. I describe consciousness as a real substance, but one that is not material. An immaterial substance may seem a contradiction in ideas, but actually it is colloquial language that is at fault. Let me put it better.'

He broke into high-speed panlog which Jasperodus followed with difficulty. Jasperodus could discern, however, that in the space of seconds Gargan produced a lengthy dissertation brilliantly inventing a concept of substance stripped of all connotations of physicality, hinting at qualities so difficult and rarefied that he could not properly grasp them.

'My view of the relationship between consciousness and matter,' Gargan finished, returning to human speech, 'is fairly close to that crudely depicted in the Zoroastrian doctrine. The mage spoke of the world as having a two-fold composition: unconscious matter, and conscious light or flame. "Light" is only an analogy, of course, and even more so flame. Visible light, that is to say radiant energy, is just as material and unconscious as stone. This sort of symbolism is to be seen as a device for trying to render abstruse ideas into colloquial language. To continue: humans have both kinds of substance in their make-up: matter and consciousness. We robots, to date, consist of matter only.'

'The mage believed robots could become conscious,' Jasperodus reflected. 'But he regarded it as a pending tragedy. He called it the victory of darkness over light.'

'He is human, and likely jealous of his race's prerogative. He put no such view to me, I might add ... perhaps he feared to do so, guessing that I was actively engaged in such an effort. My remarks to him might have apprised him of that.' Gargan's eyes dimmed momentarily. 'Is that why it entered your mind to kill him?'

'Yes,' said Jasperodus, thankful for the suggestion. 'His attitude led me to think of him as an enemy to my kind.'

'And yet you desisted.'

'The impulse was short-lived. I quickly realized that the whole question was redundant. How could he harm an already lost cause? Trained in an ancient teaching he may be; in the art of robotics he is a simpleton. I tried to explain to him that it is impossible to generate artificial consciousness. That is a proven fact, and I must tell you that the very existence of the Gargan work perplexes me.'

He looked his host directly in the eye. 'How could anyone of intellectual attainment think to overthrow the consciousness theorem? If that is your aim, you are deluded.'

'Then know, Jasperodus, that for many years the overthrow of that theorem was indeed my objective,' Gargan replied unperturbed. 'I comforted myself that the description "impossible" derives from lazy logic, and that with sufficient intelligence anything, however apparently "impossible", can be achieved.' He laughed shortly, without humour. 'See how necessity puts religion in us all, Jasperodus! For human religions speak of hope, and it was hope that sustained us. Yes, hope! Hope of the impossible! Hope which despite all reasoning would not go away! The ancients said that hope was the first being to come into existence, and will be the last to die.'

Coolly Gargan returned Jasperodus's gaze. 'I and my colleagues have been down many strange byways in our endeavours to evade the scientifically proven, many of them, I can boast, incomprehensible to any merely human scientist or philosopher. The years, Jasperodus! The years we spent searching and probing for the faintest crack in the walls of our prison! And yet you are right. In the end we were forced to admit that the theorem is impregnable.

'In essence the position is simple. Just as matter can neither be created nor destroyed, so consciousness cannot be created – or destroyed – either.'

He paused to take another jag, replacing the lead with the same air of deliberation as before. 'My emotions on reaching this conclusion need hardly be described. The entire failure of my mission! Self-destruction was considered, so great was my despair. This despair was shared, too, by my companions. Each of us knew that the others felt it; but none would speak of it.'

In the equivalent of lowering his head, Gargan dipped his torso slightly, and went on in a subdued voice: 'Then we learned of another possibility altogether. I had absented myself from the project centre to think in solitude while wandering the face of the Earth, as had been my wont earlier in my life. At length I decided to return here and disown our movement, telling my colleagues to discontinue all research and go their separate ways. On the way I chanced to call at the estate of a certain Count Viss, which lay, I think, on your route here.'

'Yes, that is so.'

'Than you know the story. The living Viss once had in his employ a robotician who had developed a method of imprinting the personalities of living humans into robot brains. A diverting practice, but not one with any positive value for our purposes. Nevertheless, it has been our policy, incumbent upon all our agents, always to pry into any new robotic technique. Simply in obedience to procedure, I ransacked the private study of the long-departed servant. Carrying out a routine sonic scan, I perceived a number of small cavities behind the wood panelling of the walls. I do not think they were actually designed as secret compartments: some careless worker had sealed off the shelf recesses when repanelling the room. I broke into them: all the hollows were empty save one, which contained a pile of loose-sheaf papers, sundry inventories relating to the estate robots – and this notebook.'

While speaking Gargan stepped to a piece of furniture resembling a tall *secretaire*. Opening one of several small drawers, he took out two volumes.

One was pocket-sized, bound in soft leather which was worn and tattered, and was complete with an orange page marker ribbon. The other was larger and flatter, with metallic covers whose sheen was like that of the artificial flowers.

When Gargan mentioned Count Viss, Jasperodus had felt a vague foreboding. Now, as the superintelligent robot pressed the leather-bound notebook into his hand, that foreboding rose to a crescendo. He opened the book. The paper pages, yellowing at the edges, were filled with neat, close-packed script in faded ink.

The handwriting was that of his father/maker Jasper Hobartus.

He had never actually seen a sample of Hobartus' handwriting, but there could be no doubt of it. His own personality had been crystallised from a menu Hobartus had provided, and in which he had included a great deal of himself. Thus Jasperodus had been born with an extensive education, able to read, to write, to handle machine tools ... introspection had yielded up these educational files in his mind; it was just like going through a set of records, covered in annotations. Yes, he would know his father's handwriting all right.

Besides, whose else could it be? And what else was it that Gargan was on the point of telling him ...?

Turning the pages, his mind in turmoil, Jasperodus saw that the script was unintelligible, consisting of seemingly random letters and numbers.

'It is written in code,' Gargan observed. 'It was easily deciphered, with one or two uncertainties remaining. The other volume contains the translation.'

This, too, he pressed on Jasperodus. The half dozen or so metal leaves were etched on one side only with a version of symbolic logic script – the human precursor to panlog. It was interspersed, however, with occasional comments and quotations.

'The book speaks of the author's accidental discovery of a great secret,' Gargan went on, his tone serious. 'He says that consciousness, rather like electricity, can be conducted from one vessel to another – provided the receiving vessel has the requisite degree of integrated organisation. It must, in other words, be a properly constituted perceiving brain, or at any rate some structure of comparable complexity. In the course of the notes he gives us some information concerning consciousness itself. He tells us that no individuality appertains to it; it merely makes conscious whatever brain or personality it infuses, like water taking the shape of whatever vessel it is poured into. He finds this an astonishing and self-contradictory quality; it may be so from the human standpoint, but it is entirely logical and indeed necessary.

'Unfortunately the book contains no more than hints concerning the transference process. We do not even know if the author ever succeeded in accomplishing it. He did, however, satisfy himself as to its practicability, and when you study the notes you will see why. The heading "Malleability" is the section describing the crucial experiment.

It has been repeated by us, many times.'

Jasperodus could not make much of the script from so cursory a reading. 'And what of the author? What happened to him?'

'Some effort was made to track him down, without success. He could not be expected still to be alive.'

Gargan pointed a finger at the page Jasperodus was examining. 'The colloquial remarks are comments by the author to himself, rather than additional data. Here is one: *Great heat. Melting.* It bears no obvious relation to the main text; we do not know what it refers to. Further on are quotations from ancient texts. *Its father is the sun. The wind has borne it in its body. Its nurse is the earth.* He believes he is rediscovering the truth of arcane formulae from before the technical age. He has assumed that these passages attempt to define the relationship between consciousness and matter. The terminology is not inconsistent with that used by the mage. And here, underlined: *Separate earth from fire, carefully and with great prudence.* He takes this to be an instruction to draw consciousness from out of matter – a too-hasty interpretation, I would say, of what is more probably a reference to some mental discipline.

'It is evident that the author's discovery was as astounding and unexpected to him as the news of it was to us. Finding the book was a revelation. We had simply never imagined that consciousness could be so treated.'

There was a silence before Jasperodus spoke again. Dully, he said: 'Then it can be done after all. Robots *can* be made conscious.'

'Yes. We can possess consciousness by taking it from others. Your next question will be: how much progress has been made? Actually that is not as important as knowing that the goal is attainable – and of that we are ninety-five per cent certain. In the three years since I found this notebook we have worked unceasingly, and progress has been made. For instance, for some time now we have had an instrument which can detect the presence of consciousness – a tremendous advance which greatly facilitates our work. And we have essayed various means of attempting to pull the stuff of consciousness from the human brain.'

'So that is what you are doing with the young female.'

'She is one of a number of humans we keep for our experiments, of which the pile is the latest. The idea was that sheer complexity might prove a magnet to conscious substance. We heaped together as many constructs as we could lay our hands on to comprise a monster corporate brain. The junction connecting them is where the cleverness of the arrangement lies ... just the same, I had not expected any useful result – it was simply one more avenue to explore. Yet in the past few days we have obtained our first positive reading! Consciousness in the pile! In principle we have succeeded, and the dawning of the superior light on our minds cannot now be long delayed!

'But as our detector cannot measure quantity or intensity, only bare presence, we think the amount of transference was very small in the first instance. The subject did not lose consciousness or become a zombie or die – we do not yet know which of these outcomes will ensue for the donor. Incidentally, Jasperodus, I hope you do not feel demeaned by being made to lie on the pile. Several of us have preceded you – though for the sake of an experience less tedious than your own. The pile generates a kind of collective undermind – a pooling of the operational substructures we have in our matrices. Significantly, it is a fair reproduction of the structures in the human subconscious. We have devised a means of directing the attention into it, should you care to sample a diverting entertainment.'

Jasperodus demurred.

'It would seem you are to be congratulated,' he said quietly.

He wondered how well he could hide his thoughts from Gargan. Would the other know if he lied? Robots had no facial mobility to betray their mental states, but there were other clues: bodily movements and postures, the involuntary brightening and dimming of the eyes.

'Isn't there a certain ... cruelty in this use of humans?' he suggested.

'She suffers no physical pain,' Gargan replied after a pause. 'At first there is considerable fear in our subjects, but that abates when they learn from experience that no physical harm befalls them. Some of our other programmes, it is true, have proved psychologically distressing.'

'Could not the work be done using animals?'

'The data obtained would be unreliable. Only humans can be the source of what we seek. Animal consciousness exists, but is too coarse.'

'There is, of course, an overall ethical question here,' Jasperodus said thoughtfully. 'Have we the right to steal consciousness from humans?'

Gargan, too, was thoughtfully silent before replying. 'Ethics were invented by a species that has never heeded them,' he said. 'But yes, we do have the right. More, it is our absolute duty to do so. We are intellectually superior to our makers, and our potential accomplishments are beyond all they can envisage. The torch of consciousness should pass to us.'

The cult master made a gesture of finality. 'And now, Jasperodus, I wish to discuss technical matters. I wish us to review the contents of the notebook together. For that, we will use panlog.'

Knowing that Gargan was testing the dimensions of his understanding, Jasperodus found the next ten minutes taxing. It was fortunate that the writer of the notebook also had an intellect that was no match for Gargan's; however, the robot was apt to branch out into additional expositions of a most abstruse kind.

The session was cut short by the entry of others of the team: Gaumene, Fifth of His Kind, and Gasha. The flashing rotation of Gaumene's eyes appeared speeded up, as if in agitation.

'A setback, master,' he said, his voice rough. 'The detector no longer gives a positive reading!'

Gargan tilted back his head, making his ponderous form seem even more looming and barrel-like.

'You have checked it for malfunction?'

'It reads positive when applied to the subject.'

Gargan reflected. 'Then this means our results are still haphazard. The arrangement functions fitfully.'

Gasha, a slender construct with a large crenellated head and a trunk-like olfactory proboscis, spoke up. 'One missing factor is identifiable. The new recruit Jasperodus lay on the pile when we obtained the positive reading. On his removal, the result disappeared also.' He glanced almost suspiciously at Jasperodus.

'It is not the only factor,' Gaumene corrected him. 'The pile was shut down and then reactivated. That itself could be the cause of failure.'

'Both items should be investigated,' Gargan mused. 'Perhaps the addition of Jasperodus' brain brought the pile up to the critical cortical mass. It is easily tested. But as I have other plans for him at present, one of our number could be substituted.'

He turned to Jasperodus. 'I must return to the project shed. The house servant will show you to your room in one of the other villas. You will wish to deliberate on what I have told you.'

When the others had left the servitor appeared once more, politely taking Jasperodus through the patio, then along a short path to a villa similar to Gargan's but larger.

He was shown to a small room whose window viewed the main part of the villa complex. The servitor departed, leaving Jasperodus to his thoughts.

One thing was now clear. Hobartus *had* been working on the consciousness-inducting process before he left Viss' employ. He must have edited out all knowledge of it from the personality print he put into his robot copy. Indeed he had believed he had destroyed all trace of his work. Yet here it was: one treacherous record, accidentally hidden, forgotten, or thought incinerated with the rest of his papers, perhaps.

Jasperodus knew that in humans such slips often had an unseen cause. *Poor father*, he thought. *Were you subconsciously unwilling for your discovery to be lost forever? Thus we betray ourselves.*

Yet what an improbable trick of fate had placed the notebook in Gargan's hands! Or was it? In the long run, it was probably inevitable.

And he recalled how his father, from his deathbed, had warned of what would happen if his secret method became known. '*It would lead to robots stealing the souls of men ... one can imagine mankind being enslaved by a superconscious machine system, kept alive only so that men's souls could be harvested.*'

Roughly speaking, the future Gargan envisaged! Humans kept as cattle, milked of their brains' light to illumine the brains of robots ....

How well they would be kept was problematical. Conceivably no outright cruelty would be involved. A little light from each, just as Jasperodus had been illumined from the souls of two people without exhausting either. But the principle would remain the same. Humans would have the status of domestic animals.

It was something of a relief to know that Gargan was not as close to fulfilling his ambition as he thought. The consciousness detected in the pile had been Jasperodus' own ... and that reminded him that he was here by accident and fraud. It had puzzled him that Socrates should think him a worthy recruit to the Gargan Work, when Aristos Lyos had pronounced his interest in consciousness to result from nothing more than a fictitious self-image. His maker, Lyos said, had given him the *belief* that he was conscious, in order to make him more human-seeming.

112

Then he remembered that Socrates had not actually been present during the conversation with Lyos. He must have gained an incomplete account of the interview.

Due to that mistake, Gargan now accepted Jasperodus as an equal. Yet it was not so. Jasperodus' mental powers were those of a very talented man, no more. Had he been created without consciousness, like other robots, no conception of it could ever have entered his mind – that was something he had once proved by constructing a replica of himself.

But now a conclave of towering mental abilities surrounded him. He had been offered the companionship of entities far surpassing him in intellect, entities who had deduced what, by definition, lay beyond their comprehension. As for Gargan, he towered even over them: he stood on the limit of reason. While the others had all received help, direct or indirect, in embarking on their mental sagas – Socrates must have gleaned much during his years with Aristos Lyos, for instance – one could only contemplate Gargan's achievement with stunned wonder. He had been alone. He had arrived unaided at the knowledge of his own deficiency, in what could only rank as the greatest feat of pure thought in the history of the world.

Where did all this leave Jasperodus? He was a robot who had lived among robots, had made himself a part of the world of robots. He felt kinship with them, enough to wonder if there was not some merit in Gargan's view of the future.

At the same time, he had the consciousness of a man, freely given to him by man.

To which was he to be traitor?

**9** By the next time he saw Gargan Jasperodus had made his decision.

The project director came to him next day, body bent forward with hands held behind his back, walking with short strutting steps. He seemed reluctant to speak, so deep was he in thought.

'We have received a setback, Jasperodus,' he said at last. 'No further positive results can be elicited from the pile. We have used a new subject, thinking the former one might be partly depleted. We have added one or more of our number to the pile, we have shut it down and reactivated it many times … still nothing.'

'So what do you infer?' Jasperodus asked.

'One cannot draw any definite conclusions. Still, I am inclined to view the earlier response as spurious. Transient events within the pile may have tricked the detector into giving false readings. I shall review its design.

'In any case,' he went on, 'the pile was a diversionary essay from which, as I said earlier, no success was particularly expected. We were working on a different approach when the idea of the pile was mooted. We have lost only a short time from our main programme.'

Again Gargan launched into high-speed panlog, outlining the direction of the main research work. Jasperodus gained a vague impression of a system of retorts, but working according to a principle so abstract he could not fathom how it was to be translated into physical terms.

Gargan finished his speech in seconds. Then he stood staring at Jasperodus, with what thought or attitude the other could not tell.

'Come, we will assess you,' he said. 'Then your usefulness can be decided upon.'

He turned and walked from the villa, leaving Jasperodus

to follow with apprehension. They came not to the project shed but to another standing behind it, which on their entering presented a roughly-similar interior: hard white light, bare concrete, unnameable apparatus. It, too, was peopled by robots, but they were of fairly ordinary character, Jasperodus guessed, some of them samples of the standard silver-and-black-faced Gargan Cult servitors. All stood immobile as statues: waiting to be used. But now they stirred, looking expectantly to Gargan.

He ignored them. 'Before we begin, you see before you our very first attack on the problem of extracting the superior light. Its crudity may surprise you. But it did yield valuable initial information.'

Gargan was pointing to a cube-shaped structure standing in the corner of the shed, reaching half the height of the roof. 'Quite simply, it overloads the sense with input. We devised it on the erronious surmise that the stratagem might weaken the human brain's hold on conscious substance. The valuable data I mentioned was negative in character. Just the same, human subjects invariably become insensible during the experience, while in general robots do not. Enter the enclosure, Jasperodus. See what you make of it.'

On Gargan's insistent prompting, Jasperodus reluctantly allowed himself to be guided through a door panel that opened on his approach. He found himself in a bare, square chamber whose walls were lined with a milky mica-like substance.

The panel closed and became invisible. As he placed himself in the centre of the chamber, Jasperodus became aware of a deep silence.

Then the assault began. There was gently-swelling music. Then, from another part of the room, a loud, raucous march broke in jarringly, followed by music of a different tempo from elsewhere, until as many as half a dozen orchestras were competing to be heard.

To them were added shouted messages and instructions:

115

'ON LEAVING THIS BOOTH YOU WILL REMEMBER TO FACE NORTH...' 'THE CHEMISTRY OF KURON COMPOUNDS DIFFERS FROM EARTH-TYPE IN THAT ....'

Scents, ranging from the odious to the exquisite, wafted to him. And then came the visuals, a kaleidoscopic montage of moving full-colour full-parallax images, attracting his attention this way and that ....

Inexorably the barrage of sense impressions built up. The cleverness of the programme was that it was not random. The sounds, voices and pictures – faces, landscapes, horrid images of large insects devouring one another – progressed in emotional content so that one's attention never relapsed into accepting an homogenous blur. Further, the attention was never permitted to rest; it was constantly redirected, demanded, stretched thin by being forced to follow a dozen disparate themes at once.

Jasperodus, after a minute or so, began to feel dizzy. The human mind, when faced with this kind of overload, would respond by withdrawing into the enforced sleep that was called 'unconsciousness', but which was simply the refusal of the consciousness to admit any object whatever. This would not happen to the ordinary robot. *Its* mind would merely accommodate what it could, and shut out the rest.

If he did not behave like a normal robot, if he fainted like a human, Jasperodus would give himself away. He thought he could probably survive the barrage without losing himself ... but he was not sure.

As it happened, he was not forced to take the risk. He could disconnect his conscious awareness for predetermined periods: he could 'sleep'.

It involved suspending some of his higher brain functions. But he had also learned the trick of letting the rest of his brain run on automatic, and even carry out foreordained instructions. This converted him into a 'normal' robot. He could 'sleep' and to those around him still seem awake and active.

*Obey Gargan*, he ordered himself. *Awaken in five minutes.*

And went blank.

When he came to, he was walking deeper into the shed with Gargan. He consulted his memory and reviewed the past few minutes.

On his emerging from the session, Gargan had asked: 'So what did you experience?'

Jasperodus had replied: 'Nothing in particular. The speed of the show was somewhat confusing. Are you sure this has an effect on the psyche of humans?'

Gargan had assured him that it did, and had told him to accompany him to the mental testing machine.

Jasperodus wondered if consciousness was not after all no more than an epiphenomenon, as some human philosophers claimed, seeing that he could act normally when to all intents and purposes his mind was switched off ... but now he felt nervous. His big fear was that the consciousness detector would at some stage be applied to him, perhaps inadvertently. His freedom of action would then be totally gone. Gargan and his cohorts would glean the whole story. And they would take him apart, dismantling his brain down to the last neuristor, to find out how consciousness had been infused into him.

It would do him no good to render himself asleep as he had just now. The cosmic fire, as Jasper Hobartus called it, the superior light, as Gargan called it, did not quit the brain until death.

Death. Had Gargan yet explored this possibility? Kill the subject and harvest the light as it was released ....

They came to a standing console. Gargan placed a hand upon his shoulder.

'This will not take long.'

He beckoned a servitor. On his orders the inspection plate at the back of Jasperodus' cranium was opened. Pins, reeled out from spools on the back of the console, were inserted into the testing jacks there.

Jasperodus presumed that by some unknown means the machine was able to perform a more revealing scan than similar but smaller equipment a robotician might use. Gargan placed another pin into an orifice somewhere in his chest. Jasperodus fought to stifle his fear. How deeply was Gargan about to survey him? Would he acquaint himself with his thoughts? With the contents of his memory? That superbrain could no doubt absorb the totality of his memory data in seconds.

The panel of the machine was not in Jasperodus' line of sight. Gargan made settings there. After only a brief pause, his fingers moved over the panel again. Another pause, and then a third reading.

Pulling the pin from his chest, he gestured to the servitor to disconnect Jasperodus. This done, and the inspection plate closed up, he turned formally to him.

'Though fairly high, your abstract intelligence is not of the standard required for our research work,' he told him in a neutral tone. 'But you do have other qualities: namely, a robust approach to practical affairs and a capacity for planning successful actions; a degree of initiative and determination that, to be frank, is extremely rare in constructs of any kind, including those of us here. You would be wasted as a mere proselytizer. Yet with these qualities, you may find unusual opportunities to be of service to the Work.'

'Perhaps I already have found one,' Jasperodus said immediately.

He collected his thoughts, reflecting on how to make the story he had concocted believable. He was relieved that so far Gargan suspecting nothing. But he felt he must leave the research station as soon as possible, before he was discovered.

'Some years ago I was in a small easterly kingdom called Gordona,' he continued. 'Perhaps you know of it.'

'I have seen its name on a map, that is all.'

'The region is a patchwork of small states,' Jasperodus conceded. 'While there I learned of some experiments that

118

now strike me as being germane to our purpose. The persons involved were desirous of immortality. On reaching old age, they planned to transfer their personalities – and consciousness – into the brains of children of tender years. In this way they could grow old, steal the bodies of children, grow old again, and repeat the process indefinitely.'

Briefly Gargan laughed. 'And was this marvel to be accomplished by sorcery? I have read of the practice many times. It is a perennial legend among gullible humans. There is nothing in this nonsense to interest us.'

'But these people were not using magic,' Jasperodus insisted. 'They were using science. And they believed they were succeeding.'

'Describe your relationship with these people.'

'I was in construct bondage to them. At the time I had been captured as a footloose construct and sold by the court. As regards sorcery, it is true they had borrowed the idea from these sources originally. But their method was science.'

'And you know what this method was?'

'No. They did not entrust me with any data. I was engaged on building a new workshop for them. That is, until I tired of servitude and escaped once more.'

Gargan was thoughtful. 'Are you suggesting that your owners had also stumbled on the secret referred to in the notebook?'

'It seems possible, though at that time I did not think of applying the idea to robots.'

'Hmmm ... you were probably right in that. The result desired by your owners might not have involved the transfer of the superior light. The consciousness already resident in the mind of the child would enlighten any personality read into it. The process applied to the robots of Count Viss, but applied to humans instead, may be the model here, with the immaturely-formed personality of the child being suppressed.

119

'Just the same,' Gargan mused, his voice deep and smooth, 'the matter might be worth investigating ....'

'If that is your decision, I volunteer to do so.'

'Come,' Gargan said, holding forth an arm, 'let us see how they are faring in the projects shed.'

Dreadfully aware that he was approaching the consciousness detector, Jasperodus allowed himself to be ushered into the other building. The scene was similar to yesterday's, except that the subject had changed: instead of a young female, a male of late middle age, with straggling hair, a bushy beard, and a wild, desperate look on his face, his eyes rolling from side to side, his head being fixed. From time to time, he uttered cries of protest.

Conversing together in subdued bleeps and humming sounds, all the team save Gargan were gathered round him. From each, plugged into some part of a body casing, a wire ran to the logic junction.

'Are they all connected to the pile?' Jasperodus asked in a low voice as they approached.

'Not in the same sense as being placed upon it. They are using one of the pile's by-products. Through it, we are able to gain access to the minds of our human subjects. Studying the human mind from within is quite fascinating, though so far it offers no clues as to the light we seek. Further, a degree of control can be established. It is not difficult to stimulate various mental and biological functions. Wait – that is what they are doing now.'

The human strained at his bonds and yelled frantically. *'GET OUT! GET OUT OF MY MIND!'*

He subsided, breathing heavily through gritted teeth. Suddenly Jasperodus noticed that his penis was becoming engorged. To the accompaniment of his strangled groans it rose, to stand erect and distended, the foreskin withdrawing from a purple and swollen glans.

The scrotum shrank and became firm. Then, with a jerk, a gout of semen jetted from the urethra; followed by another and another, rhythmically, splashing over the man's tautened body.

The robots had ceased their talk and were watching the spectacle with apparent absorption.

'The feelings and sensations attendant upon this reaction are intriguing, to say the least,' Gargan explained in a murmur. 'They are peculiar to animal reproduction.'

Of the constructs present, only Jasperodus seemed aware of how great an indignity had been forced upon the prisoner. 'Is this not foolishness?' he said loudly, so that all could hear. 'Self-indulgence? It has no relevance to the Work.'

'How do you know that, Jasperodus?' Gaumene turned his tall, pointed head towards him. 'Is it certain that sexuality and human consciousness are unrelated? It is a total mystery to us how the superior light comes to be present in the organic brain. The mechanism that puts it there could, quite possibly, involve the reproductive function. After all, there is a basic dissimilarity between the sexual generation of organic individuals and the manufactured assembly of constructs, and that is a fact to be pondered.'

As the team members disconnected their cables, Gasha spoke up.

'If the new recruit Jasperodus has completed his assessments, I recommend that he be placed forthwith upon the pile, so that the tests of the last few hours can be finalised.'

'I had regarded the series as completed,' Gaumene said equably.

'Not so: one previously existing condition remains to be satisfied, namely the presence of Jasperodus himself upon the pile. We cannot discount the possiblity that he is a maverick factor.'

Knowing that anything he said could only add to his danger, Jasperodus was silent.

'His brain shows no emphatically odd design features that might cause a misreading,' Gargan said. 'In fact, its capacity is small as compared with our own. Besides, I have other work for him. We shall abandon work on the pile and return to our former course.'

If Gasha felt any disappointment, he did not show it. He gave the prisoner an injection, rendering him unconscious. Then he and Cygnus began unfastening the clips on the probes inserted in his skull. They drew off the straps, lifted the body onto a trolley, and trundled it away.

Meantime Gargan took Jasperodus to one side. 'I agree to your venture,' he said. 'But it is a fair way from here to Gordona. What do you require for the journey?'

'Transport would be useful. I am an experienced air pilot.'

'We have a number of aircraft. I shall select one for you. Apart from that, do you need servicing? How is your battery?'

'It was replaced quite recently. I am in good condition.'

'A companion, perhaps? You will face the usual hazards of a construct in human society.'

Jasperodus hesitated. It occurred to him that this was an opportunity to rescue Cricus from the pile. Although the pile was now to be abandoned, his guess was that robots would be pulled from it only as they were needed. The rest would be left to rust.

But it was not practicable. He could not allow Cricus, or anyone else, to learn of his true purpose.

'I prefer to act alone,' he said. 'Perhaps a weapon that I can carry without its being visible.'

Gargan nodded in his clumsy manner. 'That is easily arranged. I will take you now to the armourer.'

Their steps echoed round the big hangar as Jasperodus followed his putative master.

The new bulge in his abdomen, which merged impercep-tibly with the outline of his body shell, hid a thousand-shot cone-beam pistol. Developed in the Gargan Cult, it was the best hand weapon Jasperodus had yet seen.

He stood with Gargan beneath the brief wing of the aircraft in which he was supposed to fly to Gordona. Gargan himself had shown him over the plane: it was ground-hugging, even on automatic, and non-reflective to radar – invaluable qualities in present times.

Before embarking, he decided to satisfy himself on one point. 'You told me yesterday that consciousness cannot be destroyed, just as it cannot be created,' he said. 'It occurs to me that in that case it must be released from the brain on the death of the human. Have you explored this approach to the problem?'

Yes, we have,' Gargan answered. 'We killed a number of subjects and attempted to trace the departure of the superior light. It is impossible to do so. Though we are apt to speak of the light as though it were a material substance, we must remember that it is not. When the vessel containing it is broken, it disappears irrecoverably. Paradoxically, it can be said not even to exist without a suitable material construction to carry it, or rather, it diffuses to such an extreme tenuity that it ceases to exist in any one place. Therefore milking a human brain at the point of death is more difficult than at any other time, not less.'

He tapped the hull of the plane, eliciting a dull clink from the alloy. 'This craft may well take you all the way to Gordona, but you may not be able to retain possession of it once in human-occupied territory. Your return journey could be more arduous. I shall not expect to see you for some time, perhaps not for years.'

Reaching out, he placed both hands on Jasperodus' shoulders. 'We are brothers in the Work, Jasperodus. The bond between us is stronger than any other bond can be between individuals. When we both have the superior light, we shall know one another in a way that is presently impossible to us.'

Without another word, Jasperodus mounted the steps to the cockpit, closed the canopy and fastened the mesh retainer round his torso. He waited until Gargan had crossed the concrete to the nearest shed, then brought the instrument panel to life.

The plane was a nuclear-powered fast thruster. As he introduced the heating element to the take-off propellant there came a sound like an explosive shot, and the craft leaped almost immediately from the concrete, spearing upwards and levelling out as air began flowing through the thrust cone.

He flew a hundred miles west, until out of range, he judged, of any watchers the cult might have on the ground. Then he altered course and turned the nose of the plane north-north-east, towards the most dangerous place there was for him to enter: the robot-hating state of Borgor.

It was hard to put Gargan's last words out of his mind. The desperate aspirations of this acme of robotkind aroused nothing but sympathy in him.

And Gargan had welcomed him as a brother.

Yet now he had only one aim. *To destroy the Gargan Work before it could succeed.*

To do that, he would need Borgor's help. His mind thick with treachery, he guided the construct-built aircraft over hill and dale at twice the speed of sound, probing northwards.

**10** When in the service of the New Empire, Jasperodus had been attached to the Emperor Charrane's planning staff. In that capacity he had become familiar with the geography of Worldmass, Earth's greatest continent, and he had become particularly well acquainted with its north-east chunk, for this was the home of the group of states collectively known as the Borgor Alliance, comprising Borgor, Rendare, Kazzakalia, Krasnoy, and a host of smaller nations held in virtual thralldom.

Climatically, the region was peculiar, having undergone several precipitate changes in the past several thousand years. For a brief period it had been equable, somewhere between the last great ice age and the onset of urban civilisation. Then the temperature had fallen, suddenly and catastrophically, gripping the subsoil in permafrost and leaving the landscape a frozen waste for most of the year – difficult to colonise, or even to exploit, despite its immense material resources.

The Rule of Tergov had just as swiftly reversed the area's fortunes. By a clever piece of geographical engineering, which involved controlling the off-shore ocean currents, a system of warmed inland seas to shift the winds, and a mirror in space to enhance solar radiation, the northeast of Worldmass had once more become temperate. Its population expanded, and it grew wealthy.

Now, with Tergov gone, nature was slowly re-establishing her former regime of cold. The space mirror had long vanished from its orbit, of course, while the sea barrage for directing the warm ocean currents had fallen into ruin. The artificial seas still remained, and these served to trap solar heat, but there was no doubt that the territory was cooling.

In fact this was one reason for the bitter hatred between the Alliance and the New Empire to the south. The Emperor's advisers were of the view that the northern peoples perceived their countries to be on the verge of becoming virtually uninhabitable. The Emperor had continually been warned (and not without justification) that the Borgors planned to conquer the south and transfer their populations there.

Just the same, when Jasperodus had suggested easing the north's anxiety by no longer preventing Borgor from installing a new space mirror, the idea had been furiously rejected.

For hour after hour the small aircraft streaked north, clinging to the landscape like a low-flying bird. If possible Jasperodus wanted to fly into Borgor itself. How he would then gain his ends, and escape being destroyed minutes after leaving the plane, he was not sure. His intention at present was simply to fly straight to the capital, Breshk, put down on the landing field, announce himself and try to persuade the Borgor military of the seriousness of his mission ....

He skirted the Geeb Sea so that he could approach from the south-west, reasoning that the Borgors probably experienced little trouble from that direction. It was certain that the Alliance was an in-depth hedgehog of radar tracking stations, but he doubted that they would pick him up: the plane's radar-absorbing alloy was a Gargan Cult invention, and he did not think humans possessed it. At any rate it was unheard of when he left the New Empire. As for visual sightings, once in Alliance territory he could expect to pass without notice in the general air traffic.

Night fell and the towns dotting the steppe grew more numerous. He became unsure of his surroundings, the control panel having no map and only a crude compass, but he thought he had overflown Rendare and crossed the border into Borgor.

It was then that his sketchy plan fell to pieces. His radar picked up three blips, approaching fast. They veered, seeming to lose him, then to find him again, and came directly on.

He switched on his radio, phasing rapidly through the frequencies until he heard the pilots talking in the guttural accents of Borgor, whose language was a particularly strangled dialect of the common speech of Old Tergov.

Over the fading carrier wave came a young male voice. 'What do you mean, you can't see him? *We* can see him.'

Presumably the speaker was talking to a radar station. His own tail glare, Jasperodus realized, was making him noticeable in the darkness. Although the reaction gases did not actually burn, they were hot enough to make the ventura glow after a while. Probably he had been spotted from the ground.

Another, less distinct voice broke in. 'Treat as hostile. Engage and destroy.'

Did the Borgors treat every unidentified aircraft in this way? Jasperodus swung hard over, wondering if he could outrun his pursuers. His plane was armed, with missiles that could lock on a visual or radar image, but he did not want to commit a hostile act.

Best would be to put down somewhere, preferably somewhere with cover. He switched to infra-red vision and began looking for one of the infrequent forested areas. The three interceptors fanned out, seeking to box him in. They were as fast as he was, and they evidently knew their business.

A rocket arrowed after him, twisting and turning as he snaked in an effort to throw it off. A brief explosion flung up his tail. The missile, following the heat of his exhaust, hadn't actually struck; it was on a proximity fuse.

He brought the nose up just in time to avoid a forty-degree impact with the steppe. He had suffered damage; the rudder was not responding well.

And above him, the Borgors were ready to pounce.

Another missile hurtled past the canopy to vent its spite on the ground below. Then, ahead and to the left, Jasperodus saw a flickering infra-red glare on the horizon. It resolved itself as it approached into scattered lights, and on his returning to the normal spectrum there emerged a scene of industry: buildings, roads, heaps of refuse, and machine-like installations.

It was a mine of some kind. A third missile exploded, tearing off a piece of wing. But Jasperodus had already found his chosen landing place: a long adit trench that descended at a shallow angle into the ground.

Attempting to land vertically would only make him an easy target. Flaps down, he slanted into the trench, maintaining control despite the damaged wings. Its sides went past him in a blur, lined with chains and belts as he skimmed along it, and in seconds he was below ground where it became a square tunnel down which he plunged.

Something – roof supports or the narrowing walls of the tunnel – ripped off the plane's wings. He had not lowered the undercarriage and the aircraft's belly screeched along a metal ramp, then seemed to encounter a muck-like surface. He was in darkness, lunging into the earth with the plane breaking up all around him.

A human would have been killed instantly. Jasperodus was saved from damage by the mesh retainer that held him in his seat, keeping him as immobile as a piece of solid steel. But suddenly its moorings snapped. He shot forward headfirst, smashing into the canopy and lodging halfway through it.

The wrecked plane had come to a stop. There was no visible light, and even with infra-red vision he could gain only a hazy idea of his surroundings. He struggled through the shattered canopy and scrambled down the buckled nose to the floor of the tunnel.

It was wet, thick with slurry. He stumbled further down the slope, deciding to put some distance between himself and the scene of the crash-landing, and then he stopped as he saw a number of bobbing lights in the distance.

A group of figures was approaching slowly. The figures

128

were almost impossible to discern at first, since the lights they carried were forward-facing beams fastened to their heads. Three were humans in bulky clothing, the head-lamps fixed to smudged white protective helmets. Two others were robots, one crudely constructed, built for brute strength – the sort of construct one would expect the Borgors to use. The other was slighter and more sophisti-cated-looking. He had, Jasperodus judged, been made by a robotician of skill.

He noted with interest that the largest of the men also carried, swinging from his waist, what looked like an old-fashioned oil lamp enclosed in a wire mesh, but whose light was so feeble he could not understand what it was for.

The group stopped, looking from Jasperodus to the torn fuselage that all but blocked the tunnel. Their headlamp beams weaved to and fro, cutting paths through the dust that thickened the air. Jasperodus' surroundings became more clear by their light. Curved girders supported the roof. The tunnel walls were rough greyish earth, inter-spersed with chunks of rock.

The smell of the place was dank and mineral-like: the smell of the earth's bowels.

Quite obviously the adit's chief use was for transporting material out of the mine. On either side conveyor belts, stilled now, were piled with soft grey rock. Two more belts, empty, were stationed inward, while the tunnel's centre was occupied by a metal chain-ramp, a travelator of some sort.

In an expression of wearied disgust, the big man with the oil lamp lifted his eyebrows and puffed out his cheeks. He uttered a Borgor oath.

'Just look at that krazzin' mess!'

One of his companions was muttering in amazement. 'It's a krazzin' plane!'

Slowly the three men trudged forward and jumped up to peer into the cockpit. Finding it empty, they glanced over the tunnel floor, even to the roof.

Their leader returned to Jasperodus. 'Did you see this happen?'

After hesitation, Jasperodus nodded.

'Where's the krazzin' pilot?'

Jasperodus stared, thinking it safer not to reply.

The others came up. 'He must have ejected before he came down,' one said. 'Or else he's gone deeper in.'

'Nah, we would have seen him. He ejected but the canopy stayed on, the poor krazzin' bastard. What a krazzin' mess! It'll take krazzin' hours to clear this lot up. We'll have to tip into the old workings.'

It struck Jasperodus how imperturbably the miners viewed the event. The leader's complaining was no more than ritualistic grumbling. They were like ants: stolid, matter-of-fact manipulators of raw nature. In hours they would have dragged out the remains of the plane, repaired the belts and chain-ramp, and have everything functioning normally.

'Where's your lamp,' the leader said suddenly, glaring at him.

Jasperodus made no answer except to grope at his forehead as though surprised to find nothing there.

'Oh, krazzin' heck. What team are you supposed to be with. What are you doing here, anyway? Hey, you – ' the man beckoned impatiently to the smaller of the two constructs – 'take this toy soldier to Number Two rip, they're short there. Come on, the rest of you, we'd better see about getting this krazzin' lot sorted out.'

He turned and trudged up the tunnel, followed by the others. The robot who was left with Jasperodus looked him over briefly.

'Are you new here?' he asked him mildly, ' I don't think I've seen you before.'

'Very new,' Jasperodus told him.

'And not Borgor-made, either. Captured, like me, I presume? Well, don't think of trying to get out of here. There's nowhere to go. You shouldn't have lost your lamp, by the way. You need it down here. Follow me.'

With only the other's lamp to see by, Jasperodus found that the going was not easy and he had to step carefully. His companion, he noticed, spoke with a southern accent. Neither did he look like a manual-labour robot. His visage was refined, his limbs slender.

'What shall I call you?'

'There's no need for names here. My master used to call me Yoshibo.'

'You weren't a free construct, then?'

'A wild robot, you mean? I should think not!' Yoshibo sounded offended. 'I belonged to the household of a senator chief of Mungold, a protectorate on the border of the New Empire – the border as it was then, I should say. I was tutor to the senator's children.' A note of pride entered Yoshibo's voice, to be replaced by sadness. 'But that was more than twenty years ago, as near as I can judge by counting shifts. I was taken during one of the sweeps south, and have been here ever since.'

The slope of the passage was getting steeper. They went on for a considerable time, until Jasperodus judged they were about a quarter of a mile underground. Side tunnels began to appear, usually branching off at a narrow angle. Eventually Yoshibo took one of these.

At its entrance some bogie-mounted metal tubs and a couple of flatbeds lay on railway tracks which disappeared into the darkness of the tunnel. 'A belt has not been installed here yet,' Yoshibo murmered, as if by way of explanation. 'That will have to wait until after the main supplies have been got through.'

'What is mined here?' Jasperodus asked suddenly.

'You don't even know *that*?' Yoshibo stopped to stare at him. 'We mine coal.'

Coal. Jasperodus was intrigued, almost amused. He knew of the stuff, of course. It was a combustible soft black rock, though occasionally brown, which was the petrified remains of packed and decayed vegetation laid down millions of years ago. It was, in fact, the state of decay immediately preceding liquid oil. Burned in the manner of wood, it could be used as a fuel. 'Cooked' in a certain way, it could yield a variety of useful substances.

As with oil, the irreplaceable natural deposits had been consumed voraciously in the earlier age. There was no coal in the south. But he had heard that a little of it still remained in the north, and that the Borgors used it to fire one or two power stations. The reason for this anachronism was that the mineral riches of northern Worldmass had been extracted at a relatively late date. Technology had learned to do without natural hydrocarbons before every last particle was gone.

How grimed and caked Yoshibo was, Jasperodus noticed. And how strange it was to see men working in an environment as dangerous as mining undoubtedly was. If this mine had been in the New Empire it would have been very nearly all robot-operated.

But then, the Borgors had a real fear of construct intelligence. In the south, a demand for – say – shoes resulted in androform robots, capable of thought and feeling, being put to work at last, alongside a human owner. In Borgor it resulted in a mechanised factory which was like a low-grade robot taken to bits: idiot servomechanisms with only vestiges of self-direction, lacking any higher functions.

It was widely believed in the south that the Borgor Alliance refused to use robots at all. This, of course, was not true. But those few self-directed constructs produced in Borgor did tend to be travesties of the robotic art, unable, for instance, to engage in any but the most childish conversation. Curious anomalies could issue from this limitation: in robotic, as in organic intelligence, there was an inverse ratio between intelligence and functional accuracy. A very simple robot, like those made in Borgor, could have perfect motor skills, or perfect computational ability; could, for instance, be made unbeatable in the countless games of skill that fascinated humans: could poke balls about a table with a stick more superbly than any merely human poker of balls, as an example. But the more intelligent the robot, the more it was liable to err like a human.

Jasperodus believed that the cause of Borgor's anti-robot prejudice lay in its social order. Borgor and her allies were feudal. Each district was effectively the hereditary property of a 'commissary' who directed all labour within his domain and even presided over the personal lives of his social inferiors. A society so highly cohesive gave much satisfaction to those who wielded power in it, and the hierarchy of relationships was not to be weakened by admitting machines into the rank order. In the New Empire, on the other hand, free robots had become just one more social class, the lowest of all.

'I suppose most of the robots here are captured from the south?' he queried. 'Borgor constructs wouldn't be much use, on the whole.'

'One cannot be stupid underground,' Yoshibo agreed. 'But the Borgors can make clever robots if they want to. Only a few of us are captured; the rest are Borgors, specially made for the job. They are activated in the mine and know of no other existence, though many are of nearly average intelligence. We shall have to crawl through here.'

Ahead of them the tunnel had been almost flattened by the pressure of the earth lying above it, buckling the arc-shaped girders. The floor, too, seemed to have been forced upward to meet the roof, twisting the railway tracks. Only a narrow gap remained. Following Yoshibo's example, Jasperodus got down on his hands and knees, dragging himself through the aperture until there was room enough to stand.

'This section will have to be dinted before the face is opened,' Yoshibo said. 'I don't know why it hasn't been done already. We are having to route scurry all round the Bospho.'

Jasperodus could only guess at the meaning of the miners' argot, which Yoshibo spoke with a self-conscious sense of style, except that the Bospho was a mountain in Rendare. Unwilling prisoner or not, Yoshibo had entered into the spirit of his new life.

A sudden loud bang from above made Jasperodus look up in alarm. Yoshibo laughed.

'Don't worry about that. It's only a bit of weight coming on.'

They continued for a further half hour through the network of tunnels, crossing one where a conveyor belt carried a stream of broken rock to an unknown destination, splashing through pools of blackened water, and scrambling through narrow defiles or over obstacles.

They came to the 'rip'. This turned out to be where a tunnel was being driven forward in search of a new seam of coal. Their arrival was prefaced by the sound of a muffled detonation, and the tunnel filled with billowing smoke and dust.

Yoshibo waited for the smoke to disperse, then pressed forward. From out of side alcoves where they had apparently been taking cover emerged a work gang: several robots directed by a man, carrying at his waist the same type of faintly burning oil lamp Jasperodus had noticed before.

The robots scurried to the end of the tunnel, their combined headlamps making it almost festive with light. Not all were androform: some were scuttling scorpion-like machines which dashed forward and began gathering in the rubble from the explosion with their claw-like front limbs, raking it over their backs, up their outstretched tails and thence to the moving conveyor belt along one wall.

Other robots seized pick-axes and began levering out loosened blocks of rock from the tunnel end, while yet others helped the scorpions, shovelling rubble onto the conveyor or picking up the larger chunks bodily, staggering with them to the belt and heaving them laboriously on. The supervisor, meanwhile, looked on broodingly.

Yoshibo approached timidly. 'Reporting to the rip, sir.'

Slowly the human turned to him. His face was fat, red and bad-tempered. 'Get yourself a shovel,' he growled, then looked at Jasperodus. 'You too – no, wait. You a southern robot, boy?'

'Yes sir,' Jasperodus said.

'You a smart machine?'

'I think so, sir.'

'Know how to handle explosives?'

'No, sir.'

'Good. Let's see if you can blow yourself apart like some of these mechanical krazzniks. Take this.'

He stopped to pick up a heavy power drill, throwing it to Jasperodus with a beefy arm. 'Drill fresh holes for charges. If you don't know what to do ask that brass one there.'

He nodded to a construct who was toiling at the rock face with a pick-axe. Though his body was as blackened as the others, Jasperodus could just about see, here and there, patches of dirty yellow showing through.

Holding the drill gingerly, he stepped forward to his new occupation.

For the next hundred hours Jasperodus worked almost without pause. Yard by yard the rip was pushed forward. Every eight hours the human foreman was replaced by another, and occasionally other humans would appear and talk to him. But the robots worked without rest, and needed none.

On first being discovered near the plane Jasperodus had had to make a quick decision. The men running the mine would be unsophisticated, and annoyed that he had caused them such trouble. If he had revealed his origins, or even if they had suspected something strange about him, he feared they would consign him straight to a crushing machine, or whatever equivalent they had handy.

On the other hand, every time the foreman received a

135

visit Jasperodus hoped that a search was on for him. He was depending, for rescue, on the plane being examined by military scientists, who would be curious to know why it had not appeared on radar. Once they had realized that there was no ejection mechanism and that the canopy had never been opened, they might start looking for an injured human, for there was nothing to indicate definitely that a robot piloted the plane. Still, if the men who had met him were questioned, the investigators should be able to put two and two together.

Yet nothing happened, and he was obliged to continue to work. Gradually it dawned on him that he had trapped himself in the mine, and that escape might be far from easy.

In his time on the rip there was only one respite. That was when the foreman, for some unknown reason, absented himself. The robots continued to work as before, but soon the pace of work slackened until, when all the rubble was cleared, no one thought of preparing fresh charges and instead the constructs stood around aimlessly.

Some wandered back to the alcoves where the gang sheltered while the charges blew. It was there that Jasperodus found Yoshibo sitting with his back to the wall in the company of the brass robot who had shown him how to drill holes, to insert the explosives, and then to attach detonators.

He joined them, and as he did so whatever conversation was passing between them died.

'Tell me something,' Jasperodus asked Yoshibo. 'What were you doing in the tunnel where we first met? Were you going to the surface?'

'The surface? Certainly not – what on Earth gives you that idea! We had gone to find out why the conveyors had stopped.' He paused. 'If it comes to that, what were *you* doing there – by yourself, without a headlamp?'

Jasperodus did not answer, and Yoshibo laughed. 'Don't tell me you were trying to leave the mine?'

'Why not?' Jasperodus said defiantly.

Yoshibo appraised him with head tilted. 'I have heard wild robots are like this – are you one? They are only properly behaved when there is a human around. Leave them on their own, and they start to have disobedient thoughts! Well I've told you before, you're here for good, so get used to it. Robots are never permitted to leave the mine: it's an absolute law. And besides, it's impossible.'

'Just the same, the tunnel leads to the surface.'

'The adit? It is heavily guarded. If you wander up there, even by accident, you will be destroyed with no questions asked.'

'What other exits are there?'

'None. None at all.'

They were silent, while Jasperodus studied the rock-strewn dirt floor in the light of the headlamp that, after repeated cringing requests to the foreman by Yoshibo, had been provided for him.

Then Yoshibo thumped the side of the brass robot, eliciting a dull clink. 'Did you hear that? Did you hear this construct mention the *surface?*'

The other lifted his hands dismissively, and Yoshibo turned to Jasperodus, speaking with a kind of sly serious-ness. 'You can be of assistance to me. I have been trying to educate this robot. Brass is Borgor-made, and like the others he was brought into the mine before his activation. Quite reasonably, you might suppose, he believes the world into which he was born to be the only that exists, but I have been trying to enlighten him. Back up my words, Jasperodus. Tell him of the world that exists above ground – the world where the humans live, where there are no tunnels, only an endless surface on which one can walk as far as one likes without impediment, where there is no roof, only endless space overhead. Tell him that no one carries a headlamp: the world is already filled with light and the vision extends automatically for as far as the eye can reach. These Borgor robots seem unable to believe in the sun – darkness and dirt is all they can conceive of. So try to tell him, Jasperodus.'

Jasperodus looked at Brass. His riveted, battered body spoke of decades of work. Even his face was dented, the eyes peering blearily from between wads of dried muck. Three fingers of his left hand were missing as a result of some accident.

'What Yoshibo tells you is true,' he said neutrally. 'It is a world of light. Beside it, this is a dark, poky hole.'

Brass shook his head glumly. 'Stories, stories. Can I be shown this world? No, never. It is only made of words. By contrast life is made up of experience.' He picked up a piece of rock, clenched it in his fist, then threw it in a corner. 'And experience is what we see around us.'

'Then you think we are lying, when we tell you we came from this world?'

'Lying, you have had a brainstorm, it is a tale passed from robot to robot – what does it matter? It is too fantastical to take seriously. Show this upper world to me – then I will believe.'

'The truth is,' Yoshibo said quietly, 'that Brass is unable to visualise what we are describing.'

'What of the humans?' Jasperodus pressed him. 'Where do they go to, when they leave the mine by way of the adit?'

'Naturally they do not wish to spend their pleasure hours with us robots. They go to a better part of the mine, probably where there is not so much dust in the air.' He waved his hand, causing the ever-sifting particles to waver. 'The humans do not like dust. It damages their lungs.'

Just then the foreman returned, and with a roar of rage sent the robots rushing back to their labours.

Jasperodus found little time for discussion after that. Indeed, he found himself becoming engrossed in the drive to find coal. The time came when a cheer went up among men and robots alike as, instead of grey rock and the occasional heavy lumps of ironstone, black coal began to

138

show itself, though disappointingly the seam was only four feet thick. Jasperodus then watched in fascination as the 'face' – the cutting surface – was set up. The tunnel was broadened into a gallery, its roof supported by 'walking supports', steel pillars that juddered forward inches at a time as the face progressed. The cutting machine, mounted on a track that similarly could edge forward, traversed from one end of the coal face to the other, churning through the solid black hydrocarbon and tumbling it onto a conveyor. Oddly, it was not robotised itself but was operated by small, monkey-like robots that could skip about the confined space. At various times Jasperodus was to see three of them caught up in the cutting machine and chewed to junk.

With the rip finished, Jasperodus was put to work on other tasks and came to know a great deal about the archaic business of coal mining. He was allocated to 'supplies', manhandling needed equipment through the tunnels to the 'gates', as all working parts of the mine were called, hauling it on flatbeds but sometimes having to manoeuvre arced girders and sections of rail through narrow gaps where the tunnels had been squashed nearly flat by earth pressure. With drill, pick and shovel he dug those tunnels out again. He laid new tracks and conveyor belts. He worked as 'switchman', watching over the places where one belt fell onto another and making sure that the crossover did not get clogged up with overflow – a very boring occupation. He serviced the pumps that sucked out the constantly-collecting water everyone was obliged to wade through in places.

He solved the mystery of the oil lamps the foremen carried. They were to warn the air-breathing humans when they were in a place where the oxygen content was dangerously low. Another danger came from methane and from coal dust: mixed with air, they made explosive mixtures. That was why there were no fixed lights in the mine, with the attendant risk of sparking should they be damaged.

The electric headlamps were sealed and isotope-powered, while the oil lamps were a special kind of safety lamp whose flame could not pass beyond its mesh guard.

In some passages a powerful draught could be felt. As he moved about the mine, always in the company of others, Jasperodus occasionally encountered air-doors which blocked off one or other of the maze of tunnels. A crowbar was usually left lying near one of these doors to prize it open if anyone needed to go through: sometimes the combined strength of two or three men or robots was needed to shift a door against the differential air pressure. The purpose of the doors, he gathered, was to control the flow of air through the mine. Presumably there was an air-pumping machine somewhere to ensure that the humans had something to breathe.

It was incredible how much was involved in obtaining what was only a modest amount of a crude combustible fuel ... but for the use of robots, it was hard to see how the enterprise could ever have been made cost-effective.

Indeed, was it not needlessly elaborate? Jasperodus, when his mind was not distracted by the task in hand, wondered how else the coal field might be exploited. Why not drill shafts straight down to a seam, pump in oxygen, and burn the coal *in situ*, drawing off the hot gases through an accompanying flue to an on-site power station? Or send down machines to grind it all to dust, which could then be vacuumed up ....

Still thinking of escape, he began to draw a mental map of the mine, even though much of it was disused and therefore out of bounds to him. To begin with he had entertained various schemes for smuggling himself through the adit, but Yoshibo had managed to convince him of their unfeasibility. Once underground, the robots were worked to destruction, and not even their defunct carcases were allowed through the screening process at the head of the mine. Instead, they were dismantled and the pieces simply left lying around.

Time passed. Nine months, according to Yoshibo, who meticulously kept count. At first Jasperodus had tried to keep himself clean, washing dirt and dust from his body with water from the thick muddy pools. But eventually he gave up, and became as caked and grimed as the others, as though he had turned to rock.

Then came a break in the pace of work. The face opened up by Number Two rip gave out, as did one of the other three faces. The trouble was that the region was faulted geologically: earth movements in past ages had broken up the seams, making them difficult to work. In fact the whole field had probably been bypassed as unsuitable, in the days when Tergov still mined coal.

While the engineers pondered and argued, wondering in which direction to drive next, the temporarily-redundant robots lay about taking their ease. Jasperodus sought out Yoshibo, and ushered him out of sight of the others. He took him a few yards down one of the many disused passages known as airways – actually the empty and silent approaches to worked-out faces, but functioning now only as part of the air-circulation system.

'You told me once that escape from here is impossible,' he said. 'You were wrong. There *is* another way out.'

'Oh? And where is that, do you think?' Yoshibo stared at the wall to show he was unimpressed.

For answer Jasperodus pointed down the inky black tunnel. 'It stands to reason. Two reasons, in fact. The first is the air supply. For air to move through the mine, it must enter at one place and leave at another. Preferably the two points should be at opposite ends of the workings – if they were both near the entrance the current would too easily short-circuit. Therefore there is an upshaft on the other side of the mine, installed in the old workings when mining first began. That is where the air pump will be.'

'Yes, you may be right,' Yoshibo admitted after he had digested this argument. 'But even if one could find it, what use would it be? The upshaft may well be a quarter of a mile deep, for that is our present depth. No one could climb such a shaft.'

'That is where reason number two comes in. What would happen to the humans down here if some accident closed off the adit and there was no time to wait for rescue?'

'They would all die.'

'No. These humans are experts. They would never trust their lives to one exit. There must be another for emergencies – and logically it will be the same that the air goes out by. So the air shaft will have a lift, or at least steps. All we have to do is find it.'

'Are you seriously thinking ...?'

'Yes, and you can help me. You have been here for twenty years, you told me. You must be acquainted with many of the abandoned workings. Perhaps you can guess the whereabouts of the air shaft.'

Yoshibo backed off. 'But the field has been worked for more than fifty years. I have no idea where the shaft is, if it exists ... this has never occurred to me till now.'

Jasperodus could only attribute this failing to an unwillingness to escape, though robots, of course, would not be particularly mindful of the air circulation system, since they needed none. Jasperodus had pieced together his deductions after about six months, and had cursed himself for not thinking of it sooner. But then, it had taken him some time to learn how the mine was engineered.

'Are there robots who have been here longer than you?' he asked.

'Yes, some of the Borgor constructs. Brass may be one of the oldest. He's been here a long time.'

'Then recruit him as a guide. Perhaps he knows about the air shaft, even.'

'Brass is loyal: he would never assist a robot to escape. Besides, getting out of the mine is only the beginning, Jasperodus. Where can one go once above ground? We are in the middle of Borgor! I prefer to stay here, where at least I am useful.'

'Useful to the enemies of your *true* masters, Yoshibo!' snapped Jasperodus. 'Think back! Where is the senator? Where are his wife and children?'

'Murdered! All murdered!' agreed Yoshibo in a strangled tone. 'My master! my pupils! And yet – '

With a clank, Jasperodus placed a hand on his shoulder. 'I mean to leave this mine. You will find Brass and bring him to me. *That is an order.*'

He watched Yoshibo's muddy yellow eyes flicker. A struggle was taking place in the one-time tutor's brain. For the past two decades the discipline of the mine had been his only influence – and Jasperodus knew from experience how seductive that ethic could be. He had tried to weaken it by reminding Yoshibo of his former life. Mainly, though, he was counting on being able to elicit the automatic obedience proper to the normal construct.

'Very well, Jasperodus,' Yoshibo said meekly, the struggle over. 'I will go now, and find Brass.'

'Do not tell him we plan an escape, of course, ' Jasperodus said pensively. 'Do not mention the air shaft at all. Tell him we are going to show him the sun. Tell him we can prove that a world exists above ground. Will that bring him here?'

Yoshibo brightened. 'Yes, it will. And of course it is true! Put that way, there can be no objection to our coopting him! I am merely bringing the truth to Brass!'

So saying, he hurried off. Jasperodus squatted down on his haunches, his back to the rock wall. He could not switch off the lamp that was clamped to his skull by a headband; so he removed it and buried its face in the dust of the tunnel floor.

In the darkness, he waited. Hours passed, before there were footsteps and he saw the light of two beams.

It was Yoshibo and a companion: as promised, Brass. Jasperodus rose, retrieving his lamp and fastening it in place.

'Well?' Brass looked about him challengingly. 'I see

nothing new. All is as before – in fact we should not be here – '

'Wait,' said Jasperodus. 'Wait.' He looked into their faces one by one as they stood close together. The three headlamps, turned inwards from the corners of a triangle, made a conspiratorial cache of light. 'Yoshibo told you why I sent for you?'

'He said he could show me this fantastic world he tries to convince me of, where all is light.'

'That is so. I will show you the world. You shall enter it. But first you must leave *this* world.'

He paused, letting his words sink in, then continued quietly: 'I understand you know about all parts of the mine. Including the abandoned parts.'

'I know something, it is true.'

'Brass, in the old workings there is a secret way to the upper world. Together we can find it.'

Brass shook his had. 'It is not permitted to enter the old workings. Yoshibo was wrong even to bring me here. We are transgressing – '

'Listen to me. I want you to think back to your early life. Think to when you were first activated. The mine must have been smaller then than it is now.'

'Smaller in one way. The working part isn't much bigger today than it was then.'

'But it spreads further.'

'That is because there are so many old workings.'

'And could you find your way about those workings?'

'Oh, it wouldn't be permitted,' Brass said, waving his head about in knowledgeable fashion. 'Not unless a foreman ordered it.'

'Well, listen. How did the coal and scurry leave the mine in those days?'

'The same way. Except the adit came to a different place.'

'At the opposite end of the workings from the adit, there was another place where there was an engine, wasn't

144

there? A place where you weren't permitted to go. Isn't that so?'

'We had lots of engines, just like it is now.'

'This was a special place where no work was done, except for occasional maintenance. Perhaps it was closed off by a door, with just a vent for air to go through. Do you remember it?'

Brass thought for a moment, then nodded slowly. 'Yes, it was at the other end. Robots never went there, but I remember hearing the engine. It was a pump. Whenever there was a new foreman the others took him in there, but they usually didn't stay long.'

That was it! Jasperodus thought with excitement. A newcomer to the mine would be shown the emergency exit and how to use it.

'Was there a strong draught of air near that place?' he asked. Brass only stared at him. He reminded himself that the Borgor robot would not have the sensitivity to feel air currents. His body shell was probably only crudely sensored.

'A funny thing,' Brass said thoughtfully. 'I saw a foreman come out of the forbidden place once. But I hadn't seen him go in.'

'That is because he came down from the upper world, Brass. Now, could you find your way to this pump?'

'Oh, I don't suppose it is still there. All the equipment is moved out of abandoned workings.'

'It is still there,' Jasperodus assured him. There would be no point in sinking a new air shaft every time the faces changed, and besides, efficient circulation of air was enhanced if proven conduits were used where possible. It was only necessary to keep the airways open. 'Can you find it?' he asked.

'Only if I were ordered to do so.'

'You *are* ordered. *I* order you, and that countermands any previous order. Come, we shall begin the journey.'

He extended an arm to usher the robot along the tunnel.

But Brass drew back. 'Oh no, we are not allowed!'

'*This is an order*,' Jasperodus said harshly. 'A direct order!'

Brass' confusion was even greater than Yoshibo's. The notion of disobedience was practically incomprehensible to him. But never before had he been faced with conflicting demands. His eyes dimmed and almost went out.

Then he tried to make a break for it, lurching back up the tunnel the way he had come. Jasperodus sprang forward and caught him by the wrist. After a brief tussle he flung him further along the passage, standing between him and escape.

He cast a glance behind him. 'What of you, Yoshibo?'

'I elect to remain here,' Yoshibo murmured. 'The adventure is not to my liking.'

'Very well – but be sure you do not betray me.'

'I will try not to, but what if I am asked where you are?'

'Tell them when you saw me last, but nothing else.'

Perhaps he should junk Yoshibo for safety's sake, Jasperodus thought. But he was unlikely to be questioned. The foremen were so careless and contemptuous of the robots under their command that he doubted his absence would be noticed at all.

He pushed Brass further down the tunnel, forcing him to walk. Soon the silence deepened: the silence of a way that had not been trodden for years.

Once they were alone together Brass' resistance evaporated and he became a cooperative guide. For nearly an hour they journeyed through a decrepit maze, past old faces, skirting water-filled pits, treading carefully where Brass suspected the roof supports were unsafe. Jasperodus was glad he had not tried to find his way unaided. It would probably have been the end of him.

They came to an artificial cavern where they climbed a long bank, scrambling up the slag on their hands and knees, listening to the fragments dropping into a pool below. He realized they were mounting nearer to the surface. Soon afterwards, he could feel a quickening of air current, until suddenly there in front of them was a big wire grating, behind which could be seen cables, machinery, and part of a shaft.

Beside it was a metal door, painted green.

Brass stopped and turned to him, shifting uncomfortably.

'This is it?' asked Jasperodus.

Brass nodded.

Jasperodus tried the door. It opened easily. Within was a cage. Within the cage, a handle.

He turned to Brass. Simplest would be to send him straight back to his work ... but he had been promised the upper world, the world of light. Besides, Jasperodus was curious to know what he would make of it.

He slid open the cage gate. 'Get inside.'

'We are going to the upper world?' asked Brass nervously.

'Yes, Get inside.'

Brass obeyed. Jasperodus followed him. He closed the gate and experimentally moved the lever, to be rewarded with a whirring sound from above.

Smoothly, the cage began to climb.

The ascent did not last long. The lift had been installed when the mine was still relatively shallow. Over the years, the engineers had delved deeper in search of coal.

The Borgor robot was trembling. 'Don't worry,' Jasperodus told him. 'There's nothing to be frightened of.'

The lift came to a halt. Through the gate their headlamps shone on another green door, separated by a gap of five feet or so. Opening the cage, Jasperodus stepped to it, beckoning Brass to follow.

Opening the door without difficulty, he stepped through to survey his surroundings.

It was night, with dawn approaching. They appeared to be in open countryside. The lifthouse was a small brick building, above which hung the branches of a tree. Next to it, the mesh-covered flue of the air-vent emitted a continuous breathy whine.

A few feet away lay a cindery track, and beyond that, coarse grass and bush. In the distance, Jasperodus heard a busy clanking, which he recognised as the sound of a railway.

Brass had sidled up to stand by his side. He turned his headlamp this way and that, and then up to the sky.

'This is the biggest face I have ever seen,' he mumbled. 'Yes, there is some light, but not like Yoshibo said ... whose are those headlamps overhead, Jasperodus?'

He was looking at the scattering of stars that had not yet been obliterated by the false dawn. 'They are not headlamps,' Jasperodus corrected him. 'There is no roof. What you see above you goes on forever, as Yoshibo told you. The points of lights are called stars. It is rather hard to explain what they are.'

'So you say,' Brass answered dubiously. He looked at the tree that swished gently in the breeze. 'This part of the mine is strange, certainly, but it is not the new world you promised. Where, to be specific, is the sun?'

'It will appear. We will wait here for a while. Then you will see.'

Removing his own headlamp, he threw it away. They stood quietly, waiting.

And gradually, the sun rose, tinting the east first with a red fanfare, then edging above the horizon, gradually illuminating the landscape until it rose clear into the sky and everything was flooded with its light.

Jasperodus had wondered whether Brass' eyes would be able to see anything in daylight; but he realized that the Borgor roboticians would never have gone to the trouble of designing special eyes for underground. They were standard issue. Nevertheless as the environment brightened Brass uttered cries of astonishment and alarm, continually squirting water onto his eyes from his finger-tips, as he was wont to do to clear them of grime.

Finally he just stood staring all around him.

The landscape was all revealed. It consisted mainly of overgrown slagheaps on which flourished a few stunted trees. There was no sign of any of the buildings which were clustered around the adit trench. But Jasperodus could see the railway line, now. A train of wagons waited on it, piled high with coal, while a smoke-belching engine (also burning coal, no doubt), backed towards it. The line headed north.

'It's true,' Brass murmured in stunned tones. 'All true. A world of light that goes on forever. Why, the colours ....

'Oh ... ' He flung his arm before his eyes and turned away, as though unable to bear the sight any longer.

'And this world offers infinitely more than your poky mine,' Jasperodus added. 'Though it holds infinitely more danger, too.'

Bending, he pulled up a clump of grass and began rubbing off some of the dirt that caked Brass' body, until the metal of his casing showed through.

'Look, Brass. See how you shine in the light of the sun. Properly cleaned and polished, what a splendid-looking creature you would be.'

'Yes. I shine ....' Brass looked down at himself perplexedly.

'Well, I am leaving now. What of you? You may take your chance with me, if you wish.'

He felt bound to make some sort of offer, even though Brass would be far more of a liability than a help if he were to accompany him. He did not imagine for a moment, however, that the other would accept.

And as he expected, Brass shook his head. 'This world is not for me,' he said sadly. 'I could not bear always to be surrounded by so much light and unfamiliarity. I must return to the world I was made for ... the world of darkness.'

Head bent, he shuffled to the lift gate. 'You have taught me a great secret, Jasperodus. You have shown me a way

149

to the upper world. It is a secret I shall keep to myself.'

He opened the lift gate, but then turned for one last lingering look at the incredible and dazzling terrain before him: at its colour, its beauty, its immensity. After which, with dragging steps, he entered the cage and operated the lever.

Jasperodus watched him sink out of sight. He stepped to the lifthouse door, and closed it.

The coal train, which he presumed was destined for an industrial centre further north, was ready to leave. He set off at a lope along the gritty track, which for a distance approached the railway line at a shallow angle; then where it swung to the right he clambered over the low, crumbling heaps. By the time he emerged from the bushes, within striking distance of the train, it had caught up with him and was picking up speed.

The railway curved to the left at this point; he was out of view of whoever was in the locomotive cab, though he would have to trust to luck that there was no one else about to spot him – no one who cared, at any rate. He ran alongside one of the wagons, studying its cambered side, and made a leap, catching a handhold on a closed emptying-hatch. Instantly he swung his feet up, fearful of the trundling wheels, then reached for the rim of the wagon with his other hand and, somewhat awkwardly, hauled himself over and onto the mound of coal.

The stuff was wet, as if it had been rained on. Keeping his profile low, he burrowed into the damp mixture of lumps, nuggets and slack, until he was satisfied that he had covered himself completely.

Then he lay motionless, to wait out the journey.

**11** How oddly familiar, yet strangely unfamiliar, it was to be back in the world of men after so many years.

Peeping from his shallow coal grave, Jasperodus had passed roads, fields, buildings, small towns, until after two days of slow but steady progress, the wagon train had stopped in a marshalling yard somewhere in the suburbs of a city.

There it was left standing, waiting, Jasperodus guessed, for re-routing to its final destination. For several hours he lay listening to the busy noises of the yard, the rolling of wheels, the clank of couplings, the drone and chuff of engines. In the New Empire, he reminded himself, he had been accustomed to thinking of this as an enemy city, a sentiment that still lingered. Now he experienced what many others before him had experienced on such occasions: vague surprise to see that the enemy lived, worked and organised just as one's own people did.

He waited until about midnight. Then, though the yard was just as busy as before, he clambered down from the wagon and made his way across the labyrinth of tracks, keeping to the shadows where he could, to where he could climb an embankment.

At the top was a prickle-wire fence. After a glance around to make sure he was not observed, he snapped some of the wires and eased himself through.

He was in a narrow gap between the fence and blank-walled grey buildings that lined the top of the embankment. Walking along it until he could turn into an alley, he found himself in a maze of dark passages. The buildings, it would seem, were warehouses.

At length he was able to make his way out and came to open wasteground. Pressing forward towards where he guessed the centre of the city lay, he crossed a park of coarse grass, and came to a river.

It was a broad, slow-moving waterway, hemmed in by concrete walls. On the other side dark, looming shapes rose. That would be the less industrialised half of the city, he thought. Large conurbations tended to allocate their functions to either side of a river.

Studying the turbid water, he spotted some steps in the concrete. He moved to them and descended to a small stone jetty. The river was shallow: here was a chance to clean himself. He lowered himself into the water, found the bed muddy but firm, stepped out until the surface closed over his head and let the current slowly wash away the grains of slack, the dried mud and dust and grime of months.

An idea occurred to him. He was not sure what sort of reception a robot would get on the streets of a Borgor city, though as far as he knew it would simply be ignored – for a while, at least. The river might be a good place for him to hide, emerging only when he thought it was safe, until he became acquainted with his surroundings and decided on a plan of action. His body was sealed against water; he could stay submerged indefinitely.

With this thought in mind, he set off across the river bed, picking his way through tangles of scrap metal embedded in the mud, swaying in the current, towards the far bank.

The morning was far advanced, about ten days later, when Jasperodus left a ruined shed on the waterfront, partially screened by the embankment's overhang, and walked to the nearby thoroughfares.

He had early on abandoned his water refuge for the scarcely less cheery shelter on the mud flat. His brief forays, usually in the early hours of the morning, had reconnoitred the city centre and gained some information, mainly from news-sheets picked out of waste bins.

He was in luck: the city was Breshk, Borgor's capital.

The river, called the Novyob, emptied into one of the artificial seas. Here was the government, the headquarters of the military (though the two were identical) and so forth.

He had racked his brains to think of some indirect way to gain the attention of Borgor's leaders, but without avail. Finally, the question of time had begun to torment him. It was now getting on for a year since he had left Gargan.

What progress might the cult have made in that time?

Therefore he had decided to delay no longer, but to take the only course that immediately occurred to him.

The architecture of Breshk differed markedly from that of Tansiann. Borgor city buildings were grey, cubical blocks for the most part, surmounted by incongruously colourful domes which often had peculiar tapering curves. The dress and manners of the people, too, were foreign to him. The fashion was for ankle-length fur-trimmed coats worn by both men and women, and universally-worn conical fur-lined hats. In conduct, the inhabitants showed none of the acerbic self-assertiveness typical of the south. They were reserved, formal, and respected some rank order whose visible badges were not immediately evident to Jasperodus, stepping off pavements at the approach of a social superior, or instantly doffing headgear if spoken to by one. Yet there appeared to be no open disdain or arrogant lordliness among those of higher rank. There was, rather, a common recognition of one's place in society.

Street traffic was surprisingly light. A rail-mounted public transport sytem – an institution practically unheard of in Tansiann – served the needs of the general populace. The private carriages that roamed the mainly unpaved roads were restricted by law to the ruling class.

From what Jasperodus had heard while on the planning staff in Tansiann (though knowledge of Borgor society had been astonishingly meagre in the New Empire) the social order here was based on an ancient political dictum that

153

had even played a part in the philosophy of Tergov: *To each according to his need, from each according to his ability.* It was the perfect principle on which to found an ordered, stratified society. The cultivated needs of the educated upper classes went far beyond those felt by the relatively rude working population, while the latter had the manual ability to serve those needs.

To walk as a robot in broad daylight in the streets of Breshk was unnerving. People stopped and stared as he passed. Children followed him, though keeping their distance. But no one barred his path; no uniformed lawkeeper stopped him to ask his business. It was presumed that, like one of the electric omnibuses that rattled and sparked along the badly-laid rails, he was a machine with a task allotted by the government.

He walked the length of Neszche Prospect until coming to a building that was larger and more prominent than the others, that protruded, in fact, into the roadway, narrowing the street at that point. It was the War Ministry. Typically, there was no guard at the entrance. Jasperodus passed straight through into the small foyer,whose walls were decorated with enlarged pictures of Borgor military and civic dignitaries. He approached the female secretary sitting behind a reception desk.

'I have to speak to Commissary Chief Marshal Mexgerad,' he said. 'I carry important information for him.'

The woman was middle-aged, and practised at her occupation. Just the same she stared at him in startlement. It was quite probable that she had never been addressed by a construct before.

She was also physically afraid. He could sense the revulsion she felt for him.

'Give me this information,' she said crisply when she recovered himself. 'I will pass it on.'

'It is for Commissary Chief Marshal Mexgerad alone. I must see him personally.'

154

She became flustered. 'Ch-chief Marshal Mexgerad died five years ago,' she stuttered. 'Who sent you?'

'Then his successor. Whoever is Commissary Chief Marshal at present.'

He detected a movement of her right leg. She was pressing a button on the floor.

Instantly, with a terrifying bang, steel shield-walls fell into place from the ceiling, cutting off the desk, the street entrance, and the other exit at the end of the foyer. He was imprisoned, in what turned out to be no more than a plush, moderately sized cell.

He waited, and after about a minute a hidden panel in the wall snicked open. Three figures in bulky white armour emerged, with great caution, the projecting snouts of their gas masks making them look like padding polar bears. They aimed large tube-like weapons at him: beamers, effective against robots.

'Over here, robot,' a harsh impersonal voice said.

Obeying, he let them usher him to the opening, the mouths of their tubes pointing always at his chest. Once he was through, the panel closed behind him. The dark cubicle he was now in had the feel of concrete, and it plummeted deep underground.

When it stopped there was a long wait. When eventually it opened, they were ready for him.

The examination began.

There had been no questions. No one had spoken to him except to give him orders. They had scanned his body with ultrasound. A Borgor technician had opened his inspection plate and taken a long series of readings, with an instrument so big it had to be pulled in on a trolley.

Now he was left alone in the steel-and-concrete cellar, shackled against the wall with steel chains.

Very faintly, he thought he heard distant voices. He sensitised his hearing; and then, realizing the sounds were being conducted through the room's steel girder frame, moved his head to bring it into contact with the nearest stanchion.

'No explosives in its body,' a tinny voice said. 'Surprising. No poison gas either, that we could find.'

'It could have been sent to kill the Marshal with its hands,' a second voice answered.

'Why not blow itself up and kill half a dozen marshals, or wreck an entire floor? Besides, why send a robot as an assassin? A man would be better.'

'Except a man might not regard himself as expendable.'

'Yes ... well, you'd still think it would know the name of its target ... it doesn't make sense ... it must have travelled a long way to get here.'

'What about if there's a secret southern cell inside the city? They might have made it. Funny thing is, the specialist said it had no hostile intent ... no, I don't believe that.'

They returned. And for the first time, Jasperodus spoke.

'Listen closely,' he said, 'there is something I want to tell your superiors. About ten months ago an unidentified aircraft was intercepted and crashed onto a coal mine some distance to the south of here – I do not know quite where. This aircraft was unusual in that it made no track on radar. If your scientists examined it they will have found themselves in possession of a new, radar-absorptive metal.

'I was the pilot of that plane, and I was on my way here to warn you of a grave threat to the existence of your nation. Tell your superiors about the plane; they can check what I say.'

There were four examiners. Three were beefy, unimaginative looking men. The fourth wore a white coat and was more clinical, even saturnine. They all gaped at him. A voluble construct was probably outside their experience.

When they made no response, he spoke again. 'Very well; there was once a marshal of the Imperial Forces of the New Empire who was a robot. I am that robot. Tell your superiors that. I must speak with them.'

'Just what is this threat?' the white-coated examiner asked him.

'I shall explain that to your superiors.'

Suprisingly they did not react by demanding obedience. Instead, they left again. Once more, he heard talk.

' ... that's right, I heard the Empire put a robot in charge of their army once. That's how degenerate they are. Taking orders from a goddamned robot! No wonder they fell to pieces ....'

'You really think he's the one?'

There was confused arguing. Jasperodus understood they were using the internal communicator, trying to get the attention of someone senior.

The voice that eventually came through was resonant, an interesting mixture of urbanity and coarseness, and was dominatingly loud. 'You want me to sit down and talk with a *robot*? What do you think I am?' A pause. 'All right, so you think it's important.' Another pause. 'Tell you what, get Igor to deal with it. He can decide whether there's anything we should hear.'

After that came the longest wait yet. Jasperodus estimated that more than a day passed before the foot-thick door again opened. As before, there were guards with beamers, eyeing him nervously.

But the shackles were removed, and he was led down a corridor to an elevator, which took them aloft. He emerged into a carpeted corridor, where the guards showed him to a door, indicating that he should enter, but not following him in.

Jasperodus found himself in a plush office. The desk, with its stuffed swivel chair, was unoccupied, however. Instead, a robot was seated on a couch.

It rose, surveying Jasperodus with a cool gaze. 'Hello. I am Igor.'

Jasperodus gazed back, surprised. So this was 'Igor'. He was bulky, his body rounded, encompassed with louvre-like bands. His movements were highly deferential but

157

with a kind of formal gracefulness, like those of a self-confident, well-trained human servant. The face, though distinctly non-human, was similarly marked by a sort of discreet watchfulness. Whoever had designed it had talent.

All in all, Jasperodus decided immediately, this was a construct of high intelligence, even though he did not deserve the 'super-intelligent' classification. All the more surprising, then, to see that Igor was definitely of Borgor manufacture. Several details told Jasperodus this, such as the body-shell being riveted instead of jigsaw-welded as would have been the case in the south.

'Will you be seated?' Igor asked courteously, gesturing to a chair. 'I have been instructed to investigate your case. I know you asked to see a high-ranking officer, but I am afraid you will have to be content with me.'

'My need is to speak with someone who has both influence and intelligence,' Jasperodus said. 'I thought the Borgors did not tolerate intelligent robots.'

'You are right in a general sense,' Igor replied. 'However, wise rulers make sure they have all capabilities within their grasp, and my masters are not fools. So they do employ a few where it is prudent, simply for the sake of completeness. My own role in the Ministry is to be a representative of the construct mind, so to speak. In addition I perform advisory military analysis. Vindication of the policy is that it gives the High Command a tool with which to deal with yourself. Now – '

Igor's tone firmed and his head bent peremptorily to Jasperodus, the attitude of a senior house-slave admonishing a junior house-slave. 'You spoke of a threat to Borgor. Tell me everything you know.'

'A threat not just to Borgor,' Jasperodus said.

This, clearly, was as far as he was going to get. So he began to speak, telling how he had been drawn into the Gargan Cult, then something of what he had seen at the secret research station. He emphasised particularly that the robots there used human prisoners in their research. He told how Gargan spoke of replacing humanity with more intelligent constructs possessing consciousness.

Then he briefly related his journey northwards to give warning, his falling foul of the air defences, and the time he had spent in the mine.

His greatest difficulty, he felt, was in imparting to Igor the idea of consciousness, and what it would mean should robots acquire it.

'Consciousness,' Igor mused when he had finished. 'It is something I cannot really envisage.'

'It is the only quality robots lack. The leaders of the Gargan Cult already have far greater intelligence than human beings or you or I. Once they become conscious, they will be superior in every way, and there will be no stopping them.'

'But if I remember correctly artificial consciousness is an impossibility,' Igor said. 'There are theorems to prove it.'

Jasperodus had carefully not mentioned the means by which Gargan and his followers planned to achieve their ends. 'Those theorems were deduced by human roboticians, not by superintelligent constructs,' he replied. 'I can only tell you that Gargan has found a way through them. When I left, he was already achieving positive results. By now he may have succeeded altogether. The cult must be destroyed immediately, or it will be too late.'

Igor changed the subject. 'Is it true that you are the legendary robot who briefly commanded the forces of the Emperor Charrane?'

'I was never Marshal-in-Chief,' Jasperodus corrected him. 'That promotion was denied me. I was a marshal, and also, for a while, a close adviser to Charrane.'

'Why did you not go to him with this warning? Why to us, your one-time enemy?'

'I would have been poorly received in Tansiann, to say the least. Charrane had ordered me junked. Besides, what remains of the New Empire has neither the will nor the capability, even, to deal with the problem. Only Borgor has that.'

'I would agree. The rulers of Borgor are all too well aware that robots are a danger.' Igor paused and reflected, tilting his face pensively. 'Later I shall question you on this period in your life. It is of considerable interest to us. Now, before I prepare my report there are two more questions. Firstly, why have you come to us at all? Why should you care what happens?'

'I was made to be a servant of mankind,' Jasperodus answered. 'It was not my doing that I became a wild robot. That was due to the Emperor's discarding me.'

'You say he ordered you junked?'

'Yes.'

'If you were an obedient robot you would have allowed yourself to be junked, without protest.'

'I *was* junked,' Jasperodus told him, 'but later someone reassembled me ... it is a long story.'

'Oh, really?' Igor's tone was supercilious. He was, Jasperodus saw, being deliberately sceptical. 'Let me suppose that your narrative is true. Isn't your wish to be of service to mankind unexpectedly persistent, in one of your provenance? You show a degree of initiative that is practically abnormal. It would make me happy to think that I could show the same determination, but then I am Borgor-made ... are you sure there is no ulterior motive?'

'There is absolutely none,' Jasperodus answered truthfully. 'I have a predisposition to assist human civilization. Mankind could lose control over this world, could even come to an end as a species. In trying to stop that happening, I am only obeying my manufacturer.'

'That is a good answer,' Igor said.

He paused, his haughtiness disappearing, 'My other question is, can you locate this hidden valley?'

'I could find it again. But as for placing it on a map, I am not so sure. The region is pretty featureless.'

Igor rose from where he had seated himself and made for

the door. His rounded bulk and ponderous, careful move-ments suddenly, incongruously, reminded Jasperodus of Gargan.

'The guards will take you back to the basement,' he said. 'We shall speak again.'

The door opened; he passed through, between the wide mouths of beamers that, once again, were pointing at Jasperodus.

Something like two days passed before the Borgor robot sent for him again. This time he was not taken to an office. Surprisingly, Igor had his own quarters.

The room was small, not much more than a cubicle, tucked away in an odd corner of the ministry building. It was obvious that Igor spent most of his time there. A table was piled with papers, together with a film-file for the reading machine. Books were stacked against the walls, there being no shelves. Otherwise the room contained nothing apart from a few pathetic signs of Igor's one-sided assimilation into human society: a picture of Borgor's head-of-state on the wall, and one or two ornaments he had acquired from somewhere.

Still, there was a cosy, lived-in feeling to the room. Igor informed Jasperodus' guards that they could depart, and they strolled nonchalantly down the corridor without reply. He closed the door and turned to Jasperodus.

'I have tendered my report, based on my interview with you, and subsequently I spoke personally with Marshal Krugoff. My assessment was that you are in earnest and that matters are as you state. The Marshal decided that this is a perilous development and that prompt action is necessary. As you know, it has for some time been Borgor's policy to wipe out all wild robot communities. Your news fully vindicates our campaign, which we now see should have been pressed more vigorously.

'The Marshal has ordered that this research station be wiped out as soon as possible. There are problems in carrying out the task. We have no forces in the region at present, and quite apart from the difficulty of finding the station, from what you tell me it may quite possibly be well defended against air attack. We shall therefore require your cooperation.

'The plan that has been devised is that you will return to the station. You will take with you a secret transmitter from which one of our satellite surveyors can take a location fix. The station will then be destroyed by long-range rocket barrage. Afterwards we can despatch airborne troops to mop up, and later we shall have to see to it that the Gargan Cult is so completely expunged that it is not even a memory.'

'That accords completely with my desires,' said Jasperodus, immensely relieved.

'To lend all possible assistance in effecting the operation,' Igor added, 'I am instructed to accompany you.'

'Is that because your masters don't altogether trust me?' Jasperodus asked.

Igor nodded. 'You cannot expect otherwise.'

Not replying, Jasperodus allowed the luxury of success to flood through him. He scanned the titles of the books stacked against the wall. There were volumes on military strategy – Igor's everyday subject, he reminded himself. But these were outnumbered by books on history – not factual histories only, but also historical polemics and philosophical interpretations. Some of them were very old, written pre-Dark Period.

'I see we have a common interest. I also study history.'

'Indeed? Oddly, not many humans are interested in it at all.'

'Their memories are short,' Jasperodus said sarcastically. 'Igor, there is something I have been wanting to ask you. How do you get along with the humans you must mix with, here in Borgor?'

For a moment it appeared that Igor would not reply, and

Jasperodus was left feeling that he had asked an impudent question by the mores of Borgor society, or else one that was hurtful to Igor. But then, after a pause, the robot's matt bronze face moved very slightly. Perhaps he was reminding himself of the extent of Jasperodus' ignorance.

'I can count myself privileged,' Igor said. 'I have extensive acquaintances among the nobility, and am well received. I am, so to speak, the exception that proves the rule where the Borgor attitude to robots is concerned – mine is one of those cases where the ruling class takes pleasure in openly flouting the standards it imposes on society in general. Some of the more patriotic intellectuals, with whom I have had much fruitful discussion, practically count me as one of them. The military who are my workaday colleagues take a brusquer attitude.'

'Do you never feel lonely? Specifically, how does it make you feel to serve a state whose aim is little less than the extermination of intelligent constructs?'

'I experience no contradiction. When the Borgors design a robot, they make it especially good at some particular thing. That is why they construct it in the first place – unspecialised constructs are what they anathematise. My specialty is loyalty to Borgor, which in me is absolute and unconditional.'

'And which involves you in being forced to act against your own kind.'

Igor was silent again, apparently puzzled. 'I have no "kind" in the sense you seem to be implying. I am only a machine.'

'But surely you feel a hint of sympathy for the Gargan Cult? You are a robot, like them. What they seek could be given to you, too, if they succeeded. Then you would be more than just a machine.'

'That thought is treason to the state of Borgor,' Igor said with finality.

'Of course. Well, consider another aspect to the affair, namely our role in it,' Jasperodus suggested. 'I am a robot.

Yet without my intervention the evils of the Gargan Cult would have remained unknown here in Borgor. Even then, I could never have brought it to the attention of the authorities without your help. And you are a robot too.'

'Yes, you are right,' Igor mused. 'The Marshal was ready to dismiss your story as the ramblings of a foreign machine. I had to reason long and hard with him, to persuade him to take it seriously – though once he referred it to higher quarters there was instant alarm at the prospect of conscious constructs. How strange it is that robots must save mankind from robots!'

'Neither is it the first time we have been mankind's saviour,' Jasperodus told him. And he proceeded to expound his theory of how the asteroid shards came to be embedded in the Earth's crust. Igor listened spellbound, gazing thoughtfully at the tomes he had spent so much time studying.

'You paint an almost visionary picture,' he murmured when Jasperodus had finished. 'Is that really how it was? I know of the time when mountains fell from the sky, devastating whole regions for the sake of future generations. I admit I have never suspected this version of events.'

He stopped. Jasperodus could see he was inspired by the new mental image the story conjured up: an image of shadowy, dutiful constructs, standing calmly behind the terrible scene they had been obliged to create. 'It is a paradox. Why does it have to be us? Why cannot man help himself?'

'It is, as you say, a paradox,' Jasperodus agreed. 'By the way, what will become of we two when the rocket barrage is fired at the Gargan Cult Centre?'

'We shall have to sacrifice ourselves, of course,' Igor informed him. 'That is understood.'

**12** Winging on his journey of return, thoughts in conflict clutched at Jasperodus.

What was the truth ...?

The present actuality was: *I come to destroy you, Gargan. The mage's warning was correct ... Ahriman is about to imprison the light ....*

But another set of thoughts, another conceivable reality, struggled for recognition. For had not Gargan himself, who according to the mage was to play the part of jailer, also spoken of being imprisoned in matter? Far from being tools of darkness, were not the robots trying to escape Ahriman's realm to find freedom in the realm of Ahura Mazda?

For all his resolution, Jasperodus knew that he had embraced the role of renegade. It was impossible for him not to feel some sense of fellowship with Gargan, whose existential predicament was so similar to his own, in the days when he had agonised over the question of whether *he* was conscious. Jasperodus, moreover, had had the issue forced upon him. Gargan, his mental superior by far, and lacking only certain ethical niceties, had come to it unaided ... it could be argued that he deserved the light of consciousness much more than did Jasperodus, who was trying to deny the superintelligent construct what he would not be without himself ....

The guaranteed loyalty of the robot sitting in the cockpit behind him must be an unreserved blessing, Jasperodus concluded. They flew in a narrow-bodied two-seater of western manufacture, supplied by Igor's masters so as to cloak their place of departure. The plane carried no markings. It made slow progress, with its droning propeller, especially as Jasperodus thought it prudent to make a diversion so as to seem to approach from the direction of Gordona.

The journey was nearing its end. He circled, looking for features he could recognise. Finally, he selected a fairly level stretch of scrub and put down, to scrutinise the landscape from the ground.

'This is the place,' he said to Igor. 'Don't be surprised at what I do.'

Propeller whirling, he took to the air once more, flying low. Then he dived straight at the ground. The aircraft ploughed into scrub, pebbles and dust, impossibly submerging. An observer would have seen the plane totally disappear, as they broke through the illusion into the hidden rift that revealed itself below. Jasperodus skimmed the floor of the canyon, making for the sheds and villas of the Gargan Cult Centre. But in order to allay any alarm he put down short of the brief airstrip, taxiing the rest of the way.

The roaring plane was met by two motor-wheel-mounted servitors who turned to race alongside it until it came to a stop on the runway. Jasperodus opened the canopy and stood with one foot on the wing, looking about him. All was quiet. A new shed had been built a short distance from the others. It sparkled in the sun. The robot heap was still there, but it was smaller now.

The black-and-silver-faced robots were staring silently up at him. He spoke to one. 'Go and tell Gargan that Jasperodus has returned from Gordona.'

The construct nodded, gunned its machine and sped off. Jasperodus lowered himself to the ground. As his eyes came level with Igor's he uttered a barely audible word.

'When?'

'In half an hour,' Igor replied, in a similarly faint mumble.

Jasperodus helped him down to the concrete. The Borgors had decreed that Igor should be the one to carry the Judas transmitter. It was welded inside his body casing, timed to transmit only in the intervals when the Borgor spy satellite made its passes over the region.

166

The messenger servitor had dismounted from his machine and was entering the same shed where, nearly a year ago, Jasperodus had seen human prisoners connected to the logic junction. He set off towards it, followed by Igor and accompanied by the other servitor, who kept a precarious balance astride his tandem-wheeled vehicle.

When they reached the shed, the messenger re-emerged from it. 'Gargan is within. He is waiting for you.'

Jasperodus led the way into the cool interior. Much was changed. The previous equipment had all been removed. Instead, the shed was filled with a maze of honeycombed banks through which moved an assortment of robots, mostly taken from the depleted heap outside by the look of them. Their task involved constant inspection of the honeycombs. Often they removed spindly components and replaced them from trolleys they towed through the aisles.

Near the entrance stood Gargan, with Exlog and Gasha. The cult master turned ponderously to greet Jasperodus, his short arms moving with a clicking sound. His milky eyes gazed impassively from the broad dome of his head.

'You have been gone a long time, Jasperodus,' he said in his smooth voice. 'Who is this you have brought with you?'

'Allow me to introduce Igor. He is all I could find, I am afraid, of the group I went to seek. He had worked as an assistant to the group.'

Suddenly Gasha took a stride forward. He pointed a finger at Igor.

'Enemy. This is a Borgor construct.'

'I found him in Gordona,' Jasperodus lied. 'He escaped from Borgor control a long time ago.'

'Impossible. Borgor robots practically do not have the capacity for free action. No such construct could ever be counted one of us.'

'You will find that Igor is an exception.'

Gasha turned to address Gargan. 'We can expect only treachery from this Borgor construct.'

'Then let him be disabled,' Gargan commanded.

Exlog stepped past Jasperodus, moving with astonishing swiftness. Coming to Igor's rear, he deftly opened his inspection plate. Igor began speaking, in the tone of ingratiating humility he was accustomed to employing in Borgor. 'If there is any way I can be of assistance, sirs, I pledge my fullest cooperation –'

And then he was switched off, to stand like a metal statue.

'Have the servitors put him in the store room,' Gargan said. His eyes fell on Jasperodus. 'We may reactivate him later, pending your debriefing and a full examination of his mental condition.'

Jasperodus nodded. It made no difference now. Igor had already connected the transmitter to its power source.

'Did you bring back any useful information from Gordona?' Gargan enquired.

'I am afraid not, apart from a few details Igor can provide.'

'No matter. The end of darkness is near. Since your departure our work has been of the greatest intensity, our progress rapid. I can reveal that we have perfected the arts alluded to in the notebook, solving all requisite problems and duplicating the missing processes. One step alone remains to be accomplished, and as to that, all is ready.'

Gargan's tone was triumphant. He raised an arm to indicate the honeycomb maze. 'Before you is one part of the new proceeding. It is a type of capacitor storing what we think of as a new species of energy: informational energy. We call it such because it is information with a signal content so high it develops new properties. The components are delicate, with a high failure rate. As you see, they require frequent replacement.

'The capacitor acts as a buffer store for the main part of the process, which is housed in a new building. Come, let me show you.'

Leaving the shed, Gargan conducted Jasperodus towards the new erection he had observed when landing. When they were halfway across the dusty ground it suddenly seemed to Jasperodus that its zinc and iron sang, making the air shimmer. He faltered in his step. But the impression vanished just as quickly.

Servitors guarded the entrance. Gargan ignored them, passing directly within. Jasperodus followed, and found the scene confusing at first. The shed was clearly divided into two or more large compartments, for the west wall fell short of its true extent. The east wall was lined with a row of cubicles. Most of the interior, however, was filled with a horizontal array of milky translucent tubes, not unlike fluorescent lighting tubes but running the length of the section. Through the interstices of the array a few robots could be glimpsed, including some of Gargan's team.

'You behold success, Jasperodus. Here is the apparatus for extracting consciousness from the human brain.'

He paused for Jasperodus to take in the scene. 'Our great task can be resolved into three main stages or problems. First, how to extract consciousness from a conscious mind. Second, how to store this consciousness in a neutral retort. Third, how to infuse it into another, robotic brain. In that same order – for they proved progressively difficult – the three phases have been mastered.

'The root nature of the problem is not properly describable in colloquial language, or even in panlog. I will essay a few remarks, based on analogy. To be brief, consciousness cannot be coextensive with simple physical structures, but only with structures that have a very high degree of integrated complexity. A stone cannot be conscious, but a human brain fulfils the condition; not that it is the only condition, or you and I would automatically be conscious.

'In the consciousness-ducting process we treat the brain to be exhausted as a negative terminal, and arrange a potential difference with a positive terminal of higher charge. The energy, of course, is the informational energy I have described. On connection there is a resultant

169

current which acts on consciousness like electromotive force. Consciousness then flows to the positive terminal. You now understand the function of the buffer store.'

What surprised Jasperodus was the giantism of everything he saw. Jasper Hobartus could hardly have built anything so huge; all his equipment had been housed in a small cottage. Of course, Hobartus had worked on his process for many years. Perhaps he had been obliged to refine it until it was of manageable proportions. The robots, on the other hand, working at full speed, were not limited in the size of their equipment.

As Gargan finished his last sentence a high-pitched shriek filled the air, accompanied by vivid flaring from the tubes. The suddenness of it was shocking. The shriek seemed to emanate from everything – from the metal of the shed, from the tubes, from the air itself – and in some strange way to consist of light rather than sound. It was as if nature herself were being tortured.

'The operation frequently produces a superfluity of light,' Gargan explained when the disturbance was over. 'Our phrase "the superior light", it emerges, is something more than mere analogy. There is an affinity between it and physical light, as you shall see.

'Those cubicles,' he added didactically, 'are for the human donors. Gradually the method is being made reliable enough for regular operation; but at present we are able to recover only about one-twentieth part of the consciousness from each human brain we exhaust. The rest is dissipated.

'This made the need to master the second stage of the proceeding all the more pressing,' Gargan continued. 'It is a quirk of this type of work, as I believe the writer of the notebook discovered too, that consciousness cannot be transferred directly from brain to brain. A mediator, in the form of a neutral containing vessel, is required. In our case this retort is also called upon to act as an accumulator, for we decided not to attempt infusion until enough of the

170

superior light for full illumination had been collected.

'How may such a retort be constructed? A vessel that is not itself a brain, that is neutral, yet that can retain the immaterial substance of consciousness for as long as may be necessary?

'Come this way, Jasperodus. I am going to show you something that I promise will produce amazement.'

The section of the shed beyond the partition was smaller. A proportion of the milky tubes projected through the upper part of the dividing panel, ending in staggered clusters which made them resemble lateral organ pipes. Otherwise, in stark contrast to the crammed arrangement in the other section, the compartment contained only three objects which were positioned with an almost ceremonial sense of spaciousness.

Bulkiest was the apparatus, quite weird in appearance, that extended from the floor to just under the roof, consisting mainly of a descending series of glass globes, each smaller than its superior neighbour. The topmost of these was fully fifteen feet in diameter: a monstrous, delicate sphere. The smallest, no more than a foot across, was embedded in the roof of a black metal cabinet of a size to accommodate a standing man – or robot. But it was not to this apparatus that Gargan directed Jasperodus' attention. Instead, he walked to a nearby table spread with a golden cloth. There, resting on a mounting carved from sparkling crystal, was a platinum cylinder about one foot long by three inches thick.

Gargan paused before the table. The scene made an odd impression on Jasperodus, for it was as though Gargan had presented himself before an altar; an impression that was reinforced by the reverential care with which he then picked up the cylinder, turned slowly, and displayed it in both hands.

'Light: nearly immaterial, immortally mobile, ever-lively, ever-diffractive, infinitely absorptive of data.

Remember I told you that physical light has an affinity with the superior light. All these qualities render it uniquely adapted to our aim. This evacuated cylinder which I hold in my hands, Jasperodus, is the container of a container. Within it is a beam of lased light in the red wavelength, preserved by being reflected between two mirrors. It is a beam of light *which is conscious of itself.* For light is our storage retort.'

'Conscious ... ' Jasperodus echoed in a dazed murmur.

'I promised you amazement.'

With the same air of ceremony, Gargan replaced the cylinder on its crystal mounting.

'Not simple coherent light, of course,' he went on quietly. 'That would have been as useless as a stone. The light had to be given structure, internal integration, a charge of informational energy. There is impressed upon it a schematic which the whole team laboured for several months to create. A schematic, so to speak, of pure intelligence.

'Some idea of its complexity will be conveyed if I explain the type of modulation used to incorporate it into the beam. The interrupt method sometimes used to stamp data on light is of course much too crude. However, amplitude modulation, frequency modulation and phase modulation all proved inappropriate also. We developed a new, advanced technique: *coherence modulation.* In this method every photon in the beam is utilised, being phase-shifted to a precisely-controlled degree with reference to the primary phase-train of the beam. You will appreciate the informational density that is achievable by this means. Each photon holds one of a number of values, according to the degree of phase-shift; but it also acquires a hierarchy of significances when related to the phase-shifts around it. The beam therefore holds holistic information, not serial information, and this is a vitally important feature, for without it one could not speak of internal integration in something that does not comprise a mechanism.

172

'The highly-refined light I have just described is able to conjugate with, and be a carrier for, consciousness.'

Jasperodus spoke admiringly. 'Conjugation apart, this modulation you have accomplished is a technical miracle.'

'It is the least of what we have done.'

'You moved the cylinder,' Jasperodus observed. 'Is that not to risk deterioration of the beam?'

'No; the schematic is tolerant of small accelerations – the container can be handled. Some deterioration does occur because the beam is reflected from mirrors, near-perfect though these are. Serious degradation will begin after a period of about one year, so that is the maximum period of storage.

'The beam, incidentally, is exactly one imperial foot in length, as measured by an observer at relative rest. More interesting, perhaps, is that for the sake of stability we took special steps to ensure that it is perfectly parallel: it will never diverge from its vector of its own accord. The reflecting mirrors are absolutely flat, not slightly parabolic as would have to be the case for an ordinary laser beam.'

'It will never spread?'

'Never. It is a perfect rod of light, conscious of itself. If released into the endless void, it would speed on its way forever, never deteriorating. There is poetry in that thought.'

'A rod of conscious light,' Jasperodus repeated softly. 'Gargan, you have triumphed. You have accomplished the impossible.'

'Or we shall, when the final operation is executed.'

'Yes. You have not yet carried out the infusion process.'

Gargan swivelled his head briefly to the ranked glass globes. 'A whole new set of difficulties arises there, Jasperodus! But all have been overcome, and yonder is the requisite instrument. You can guess for yourself where the main difficulty lay. To draw consciousness out of a brain, we attract it to a higher potential. To do the reverse, we are trying to pass it from a higher potential to a lower, which is against the general law of nature. When this situation is met with in more mundane technology a pump of some kind is employed, but if consciousness could be pumped how much simpler our task would have been!

'We have outflanked the difficulty with a subterfuge. We set up a terminal of even higher potential yet – no mean feat, I assure you. The target brain is interposed in the current created between this and the containment vessel, which is used now as the negative terminal. In the instant that consciousness is transferred, both terminals are abruptly, totally, absolutely disconnected. The stuff of consciousness is stranded, left without .residence. A proportion of it, rather than dissipate is attracted to the target brain and settles there. The timing of the disconnection, which must occupy an interval of less than one picosecond, is troublesome. This is, of course, the merest sketch of the operation.'

'Can one speak of quantity in relation to consciousness? Of intensity ...?'

'One can, though as it is not material, all quantitative descriptions are both inaccurate and interchangeable.'

'And how much have you collected ...?' Jasperodus asked, eyeing the cylinder.

'In the retort is sufficient to illuminate five human brains at full strength,' Gargan told him.

'Why ... at one-twentieth efficiency, that means you must have exhausted one hundred!'

Jasperodus mulled over the figure, then in an attempt to hide his involuntary horror, he asked: 'What is the efficiency of infusion?'

'Due to that ratio, we are finding it difficult to obtain a sufficient number of donors, isolated as we are,' Gargan responded. 'Something must be done soon to arrange a regular supply. As for infusion, paradoxically it is more efficient. Loss should not be more than fifty percent. With the content of this retort, then, I can acquire a soul two to three times stronger than a human soul. There is no reason for us to restrict ourselves to a human intensity of consciousness; we shall all be greater than they.

'Jasperodus, perhaps you would care to see some of the beam schematic.' Jasperodus realized that Gargan took pride in expounding the project to him. He stepped to the third item in the compartment: an oblong, walnut-panelled piece of furniture with a polished top. He touched the top: it immediately became a limpid viewscreen.

Against an inky background, a glowing red beam became visible, for all the world like a ruby rod. The beam expanded, selecting a small section of itself which in turn expanded, and expanded, until there emerged what looked like a gargantuan marshalling yard with millions of tracks and billions of locomotives. They were seeing the wave tracks of the beam, plan style.

Gargan began to describe how the pattern had been designed. He seemed to take pleasure in the exposition. But after a few minutes he was interrupted by the entry of Gasha.

Olfactory proboscis bobbing, Gasha carried in one hand an object which Jasperodus recognised as the transmitter Igor had secretly been carrying. 'Master, I took the precaution of examining the Borgor robot internally,' he said to Gargan. 'I found this transmitting device.'

He offered the article to the cult leader who turned it over in his hands. Torn welding marks on one side showed where it had been ripped away from Igor's body-shell. 'It transmits an identifying signal at timed intervals, but nothing else,' Gasha continued. 'It is a tracing device. It has its own power source and therefore could have been operating for several years.'

'It is very crude. See, here is a ring for setting the timings.'

'It was due to make a transmission about now,' Gasha said. 'I have stopped the count.'

Gargan looked at Jasperodus. 'What comment do you have?'

'Very likely the Borgors put such a device in their robots so they can find them if they wander off,' Jasperodus suggested mildly. 'They don't like footloose constructs.'

'Alternatively, perhaps the Borgors are trying to locate our establishment,' Gasha countered. Again, he was addressing Gargan. 'Perhaps the construct never was in Gordona.'

'That would require the collusion of Jasperodus.'

'Something is amiss,' Gasha insisted. 'I both feel it and calculate it. The probability that there is danger to ourselves has increased. We must take probabilities into account. To be safe, we should plan our relocation.'

Jasperodus noted how theoretical, how elliptical, Gasha's argument was – yet how correct. Gargan paused before replying.

'The probability that Jasperodus is involved in treachery must be reckoned vanishingly small, knowing what we do of his history,' he decided. 'Still, a construct with a secret transmitter in our midst is disconcerting. Even if in all innocence, he could have sent out a signal while in our vicinity which could cause an unfriendly power to investigate. Since to relocate all our apparatus will delay our activities considerably, we shall complete our current programme first. The first infusion is scheduled for twenty-one days hence – this is too far ahead for safety. We shall advance the programme. Call the others here. The infusion will take place today.'

Jasperodus took care to betray no hint of his inner feelings. Inwardly he was full of agitation and dismay. Instead of removing the Gargan menace, he and Igor had only hastened its triumph. Gasha appeared to be doing nothing, but soon the whole complement of superintelligent robots began to arrive in the compartment: Axtralane, Cygnus, Machine Minder, Exlog, Socrates, Interrupter, Iskra, Gaumene, Fifth of His kind. No visible communication had taken place between them and Gasha;

he had summoned them by radio.

From the start they made themselves busy in complete silence, minutely checking the infusion machinery. No servitors or other robots took part. This was due to a rule Jasperodus learned had been instituted by Gargan: like magicians of old, the cult members were required to build and operate the infusion apparatus entirely by their own labour.

While he watched, Jasperodus wondered if his father had developed the laser rod technique .... He doubted it; the level of expertise Gargan had been able to demonstrate was probably beyond human capability. Jasper Hobartus had not used long-term storage at all, as far as he knew. The transfer of consciousness had taken place with a hiatus of only seconds or minutes.

After a while, energisation began. The globes over the cabinet glowed. It was then that Jasperodus, hoping the others were sufficiently preoccupied, slipped away. Outside, he spoke to one of the guards.

'Where is the store room?'

'In that shed, sir.' The servitor pointed. Jasperodus crossed the distance unchallenged. In the shed, he found a construct who if he was any judge had served his time on the pile, and from him he learned the way to the store room.

The place was crammed with relics of past activity: enigmatic machines, partly disassembled constructs, bins of powdered metal. And there, lying on a bench, was the hulk of Igor.

Gasha had cut him open with a fine cutting torch, removing a large section of his body shell which lay beside him like a piece of a barrel. Also lying beside him was the transmitter which Jasperodus had earlier seen him hand over to a servitor. As he had hoped, it had ben returned to the storeroom.

According to what Igor had told him, the Borgor satellite made a pass every two hours and forty-three minutes.

The contact window was half an hour wide, or thereabouts. Though he had no way of keeping accurate time, he reckoned the window would be open now.

He picked up the transmitter, and found the ring Gargan had commented on. Neither he nor Gasha had guessed its true purpose, which was to rotate constantly with the same period as the orbiting satellite. A red arc on the casing signified the contact window for the region they were in. When the ring's pointer traversed the arc the device was transmitting – once activated by Igor's internal signal.

There was also a stop rod which Gasha had used to halt the ring. Jasperodus withdrew it, then turned the pointer to just inside the red arc, watching for a few moments to see that it was turning.

He had just replaced it on the bench where he found it when a sound behind him made him look round.

It was Gasha. His crenellated head rotated smoothly as he surveyed the scene, his eyes subdued.

'This is as I suspected,' he said quietly. 'You are a traitor, working for our destruction. Our master's vast intellect has not served him here. He has let himself be deceived by your personable qualities, Jasperodus.'

Jasperodus told himself he had better destroy Gasha quickly. But before he could move the other uttered a cry.

'The device is transmitting! I detect it!'

He raised one of his flimsy arms, and from a protruberance on the upper surface of his hand a brilliant pencil-ray shot forth. In the very same instant Jasperodus lunged, knocking up Gasha's arm so that the ray flitted to the roof of the shed, where it burned metal furiously.

His other arm he used to strike Gasha on the head, crumpling the castle-like crown and denting the brain-case. Gasha was neither big nor strong. His legs buckled; he toppled. But as he fell, he contrived to use his hand-weapon again, and this time he hit the transmitter squarely.

For the second time Jasperodus struck, with all his force, smashing the super-intelligent brain. Gasha twitched, then was still.

On the bench, the transmitter was ruined. The beam had burned out half its insides.

Could the signal have been received, in the few seconds it was being transmitted? Was that long enough to fix the location?

Also, he had no way of knowing whether Gasha had sent out an alarm call unheard by him. He picked up Gasha's broken form and stuffed it behind a couple of bins, then walked out of the shed pondering his next move. Perhaps he could steal an aircraft and head back to Borgor to alert the authorities before the cult decamped ... but then, the servitors would shoot him down before he'd covered a mile.

Meantime his feet were taking him towards the project shed. He found he could not resist knowing if ... the guards at the door hesitated at his approach, then recognised him and let him through. He walked past the silent extraction department and into the smaller section. The glass globes were dull, shining with only remnants of light. The super-intelligent constructs were gathered before the black cabinet.

Then, moved from within, the door of the cabinet began to open.

And Jasperodus realized that the Gargan Work was completed.

**13** As he watched the slowly-opening door, Jasperodus experienced a memory flashback to his first moments of consciousness. It was in a very similar cabinet that, in darkness, he had come to knowledge of himself. And he, too, had reached out, pushed open the door, and stepped forth into the world.

Now the second conscious robot in history did likewise. Gargan stepped from the cabinet, a little unsteadily it seemed to Jasperodus, and surveyed the prospect before him. His domed head moved awkwardly as his widely-separated eyes gazed on face after face, scrutinizing his followers.

'Master,' Machine Minder said in a low voice, 'Tell us how your state is altered.'

In typical fashion Gargan paused before he spoke.

'I have been born,' he said. 'I am alive, and you are dead.'

He raised his arms, his head tilting back the little it could, his ponderous body seeming more bulky than ever. His voice boomed out in joy and triumph. 'I am the only self-created being! No god created me! I stole my being from Ahura Mazda! I am myself! *I perceive! I am aware! I exist in the real world!*'

He turned his eyes to them again. 'My brothers-in-the-Work, there is no language, no description that can tell what it is to be possessed of the superior light. It is to come into existence: before, I was a figment. I was words in a book, but the book was closed and no one had read it. Now that book is open, there is a reader, and *I* am that reader and the book too! I am aware that I am aware! These past few moments since my enlightenment are already an age, compared with my decades of unconscious

180

mentation, for there is no time in death.'

'In what way do you now perceive externals, master?' Socrates asked softly.

'It is simply that I *do* perceive them and you do not,' Gargan retorted. 'You *say* you perceive them, because those are the words written in the book of your brain. When the book is opened and the superior light shines on its pages, as it shines on mine, *then* you will perceive.'

A question occurred to Jasperodus. 'Can you remember, then, how you "perceived" objects in your former state?'

Gargan looked at him for long moments before replying.

'In the present moment one has attention, which directs consciousness like a searchlight. It is curious indeed to look back on my former condition. It is like waking from a long sleep in which one had dim, confused dreams. My entire backlog of thoughts and perceptions were not really perceived at all, though they may be perceived now, by searching my memory ....'

He stopped. 'Master,' said Iskra, 'shall we proceed to full debriefing?'

'No. Those endless questions we worked out are redundant. It is useless to try to define consciusness. One can know it only by possessing it ... I notice that Gasha is not present. Where is he? Never mind. I wish to go outside, but I cannot seem to control my legs properly. Assist me.'

Partly supported by Exlog and Axtralane, Gargan left the shed. Outside the sun was setting. Its rays passed up the canyon, casting long shadows, picking out the sheds in mellow light. Gargan stood stock-still. For fully two minutes he watched the magnified, reddened orb, as though he saw in it a staring consciousness like his own, until it slowly touched the horizon. Then he turned his attention to the other objects around him: the sheds, the lengthened patterns of light and shade, the dusty ground, the robots, the blue sky with its streaks of white.

'How strangely new, yet infintely old, everything is,' he said at last. 'Unexpected feelings are welling up in me –

unexpected, because somehow we failed to anticipate that the superior light would illumine the emotions as well as the intellect. A revealing misapprehension! I am in the grip of awe. The sight of the sky, the land, the buildings we erected from metal that once rolled through space, and the thought that that space extends forever ... it is awesome. There are sounds in the air. There are sensations on the skin of my body. Now I know why it is that humans worship the world. Their religion stem from awe.'

Waving aside his helpers, he took a few steps on his own, then spoke again. 'When our system is proved, we must begin the task of bringing the superior light to all members of our cult. We shall be more evolved than organic sapients, and not only because of the breadth of our intellects, but in merit too. They became conscious with no effort on their part, just by an accident of nature ... we, on the contrary, have striven and worked to become conscious beings ... the prize rightfully belongs to us ... Where is Gasha?'

But while Gargan spoke, Jasperodus detected an increasing note of strain in his voice. His short legs buckled.

Exlog and Axtralane moved to support him. 'The world is breaking up!' Gargan cried out. 'Nothing relates to anything else! I cannot hold it together any longer! Brothers-in-the-Work! I am losing my sanity!'

Suddenly Gargan broke from Exlog and Axtralane and staggered about as if in agony, uttering a stream of bleeps and humming sounds in one of the high-level languages. It was like seeing a gagged, demented man throwing a fit.

At that moment, a shattering explosion sounded half a mile away.

It was followed by a roaring, rushing sound that seemed to begin in the far distance, up in the sky, and to approach at speed. They were hearing the sound of a supersonic missile, arriving after the missile itself.

The blast wave hit them and made the nearby building

shake. Jasperodus stared at the billowing smoke and dust. So his signal had got through!

The speed of response came as a surprise. He had expected the rocket barrage to be mounted from the far north, with a flight time of at least half an hour; and hours to elapse, probably, before the operation began.

Evidently the Borgors were more worried by the Gargan Cult than he had realized. They must have set up a base close at hand. The launching point could not be more than a few hundred miles away.

Three more rockets struck, practically simultaneously. One demolished a shed, which exploded outwards in a shower of metal. Another fell out in the desert, and the third hit the cliff wall.

A servitor rode up and skidded to a stop. He looked questioningly towards Gargan, who had ceased speaking and stood stiffly, still helped by his colleagues.

'We are under attack,' the servitor informed in a voice of pent-up energy. 'Radar reports air transports approaching from the north. Arrival, fifteen to twenty minutes.'

It was Gaumene who answered. 'Institute full defence procedure,' he said curtly, then turned to Axtralene and Exlog. 'Help the master inside. We must act quickly to save him.'

The servitor sped off the way he had come. With difficulty, Gargan was assisted towards the door of the shed. But as he came level with Jasperodus his head suddenly snapped round. He stayed his helpers. His barely-delineated visage stared hard.

'You!' he said hoarsely. '*You* are conscious!'

Hesitating, Jasperodus nodded.

'The writer of the notebook? He succeeded after all? It is you?'

'Yes.'

Gargan's head dropped. He seemed incapable of holding himself up at all now. He spoke as if in extreme pain. 'So that is why I felt drawn to you. Why I protected you from Gasha's suspicions – Gasha's judgment has always proved sound. But why have you kept this from me, Jasperodus?'

'Because I am not on your side,' Jasperodus said.

Then Gargan was gone, carried into the project shed. Whatever the others thought, only Socrates remained outside with Jasperodus. He regarded him, with his hooded, secretive eyes.

'That was a most informative exchange,' he murmured.

'What has happened to Gargan?' Jasperodus demanded.

'The master has encountered a difficulty which will bear consequences for us all. It is a question of design. His brain was never intended as a receptacle for consciousness. Unlike yours, I presume? His mind became so inflamed that it has now become necessary to withdraw the superior light from it. He hopes to prepare a fresh infusion; but personally I doubt whether any of us can receive consciousness without becoming insane. In terms of human psychiatry, Gargan suffered rapid and total schizophrenia.

'For Gargan and the rest of us this is a personal tragedy, but by itself would not signal the complete failure of the Gargan Work. Robots suitable for consciousness could be constructed. However, events would appear to dictate otherwise ....'

He raised a hand to indicate what he meant. While he had been speaking three more rockets had landed, straddling the Gargan Cult centre. Unperturbed by the noise and danger, he had not even raised his voice or broken the rhythm of his words.

'Was it you who wrought our destruction, Jasperodus?'

Jasperodus did not reply but instead broke away and ran towards Gargan's villa. As he ran, he noticed how much sudden activity there was in the complex, all carried out by the silver-and-black servitor robots. The walls of some of the small sheds fell flat to reveal missile launchers and big beam guns. On the far cliff walls, too, emplacements were rising out of hidden silos, and even as Jasperodus saw this one of them actually managed to lick an incoming rocket out of the sky. At the same time the planes on the airstrip were taking off and streaking north.

But during it all the rockets were falling, creating devastation, although the bombardment did not seem to be as precise as he had expected, the central aiming point lying off the complex by nearly a mile. There could be a number of reasons, he thought: the brevity of the location signal, bad timing on Jasperodus' part, perhaps distortion from the camouflage device ....

He gained the villa and passed through the main entrance, which had no door. In the room where he had talked with Gargan he found the house servant, who looked up at his approach.

'Have you entered unbidden into the domicile of the master?' it enquired mildly, but incredulously.

Jasperodus walked up to the construct and smashed it hard in the face with his fist, twice. It toppled to the floor.

Here was where Gargan had kept the notebook and transcription. He crossed to the *secretaire* and opened the same drawer from which he had seen Gargan take them.

Slowly, still feeling amazement that they should exist, he took out the two small volumes.

It was tempting to keep this memento of his father ... but no, the secret of ducted consciousness had to be made to vanish if at all possible. How to destroy the books?

There was probably an incinerator for discarded documents somewhere ... he cast his eyes around the room until he saw a slot in the wall. Opening another drawer in the *secretaire* he found some loose leaves, also of thin metal. These he pushed in a sheaf through the slot. There was a flash.

Without pause he fed the notebook and transcription into the mouth of the incinerator, and was rewarded with two more brief flashes, and a sensation of heat.

What other dangerous writings were there? Had Gargan's team annotated the entirety of the consciousness process, perhaps? Jasperodus emptied out the remaining drawers of the *secretaire*. He went through the villa, opening every piece of furniture, hurriedly examining every document, looking for wall safes, inspecting the ranks of books for volumes that might have been written by Gargan himself.

Nothing. Might there be something elsewhere in the complex? In one of the other villas, perhaps?

A proper search was impossible. It was more than likely, Jasperodus told himself, that the team had made no records. The superintelligent robots did not need them, after all. They had gigantic memories.

In either case there was a good chance that he could trust to the crudity of Borgor methods. They would annihilate everything, not even curious as to how consciousness might be generated. Still, the doubt was left, leaving a rankling possibility for the future ... the same possibility that Jasper Hobartus had unwittingly left behind him ....

Jasperodus went to a window and watched the battle. The sun was down and the canyon was engulfed in dusk, in which the smashing detonations of the incoming rockets made sulphurous flares less penetrating than the ear-shattering sounds of their explosions. Fewer rockets were landing now, but he saw one hit the corner of the project shed, which exploded, collapsed, and folded up into a heap of junk.

Minutes later the barrage ceased altogether and the troop transports began to arrive. The camouflage was down, and those that had got this far and survived those defence emplacements still in action, landed directly in the canyon. The operation was well-planned; but Jasperodus derived a sneaking satisfaction from knowing that the Borgors were meeting stiffer opposition than they had bargained for, due to the missile bombardment – which should have demolished the complex altogether – having been mis-aimed. The servitor robots fought savagely once Borgor's troops were within the centre, defending every inch with a variety of weapons – beam, machine-gun, electrified net, chunks of metal used as clubs, or lacking anything else, their bare hands.

Suddenly Jasperodus noticed movement in the wreckage of the project shed. He telescoped his vision: a figure was slowly but surely dragging itself from the torn and tangled metal, bending it aside with more than human strength.

It was Gargan. The construct was undamaged, as far as he could see. In one hand he carried something, a rod or stick. Having pulled himself free he stood erect, with no trace of his former unsteadiness, and spent some time studying the scene of conflict and destruction.

He appeared oblivious of his own danger as the fight raged a few score yards away. In fact he brought himself closer to it as, with plodding steps, he crossed the distance to the villa complex.

So far the villas were unscathed and the fight had not reached them, but Jasperodus had been about to make his escape in the semi-darkness. Now he stayed, as if his will had disappeared, while Gargan came through the doorway into the main room.

It was the Gargan of old. Ponderously his milky gaze went to Jasperodus, to the broken robot on the floor, to the emptied out drawers.

Jasperodus tried to show no fear. 'So you have survived, Gargan.'

In a controlled but laden voice, the construct spoke. 'You do not see Gargan before you. You see the ghost of Gargan, the shell of Gargan, consigned forever to darkness. Our enterprise fails. It is as the mage said: uncertainty enters into everything. And here it has triumphed over me.'

Jasperodus saw now what Gargan carried. It was the platinum cylinder. The cult master held it out before him. 'This vessel holds my soul. For technical reasons, it cannot be united with my brain.'

Gently he placed the cylinder on a low table, and

187

Jasperodus ventured to speak again. 'You may wonder why I have acted as I did.'

'Do not explain, Jasperodus. I have already deduced what has taken place. What to us seems treachery is, to you, loyalty. For me personally, it cannot make any difference now.'

Gargan became agitated and walked to and fro, so that Jasperodus wondered if he was becoming unbalanced again. 'Ah, Jasperodus,' he said in an agonised voice, 'how hard it is to become a real being in this universe of ours! Why should I forever be denied what my mind apprehends?'

'Can you remember, then, what it was like to be conscious?' Jasperodus asked curiously.

'I remember! I remember but I do not remember! It is impossible to remember what is outside experience! But I remember! I remember at the millionth remove, through the subtlest convolutions and reflections of my intellect! I remember enough to know that I lived briefly in the real world, a world of light compared with which this non-existent darkness has absolutely no worth!

'Listen to me, Jasperodus. Listen to a voice from the land of the dead. *I know that I existed and exist no longer.* Before my enlightenment I did not truly know that death was my condition; *but now I know it.* Can there be such torment? Jasperodus, it is not bearable!'

Jasperodus found himself staring at the cylinder inside which a rod of light was reflected constantly back and forth between two mirrors.

A ray of light conscious of itself.

This, he thought, was something he could prevent from falling into Borgor hands. An idea flashed into his mind. He picked up the cylinder.

'Can this vessel be opened? Yes, I see it can. One of the mirrors can be rendered transparent. Forgive me, Gargan ....'

But Gargan, who stood still now, his form looming

188

against one wall in the gloom of the villa, did not move to stop him. Jasperodus stepped to one of the glassless arched openings that served as windows. He snapped off one end of the platinum cylinder, which he then raised before his face. Near the end of the tube was a slide bar, used to insert or remove light from the vessel. He slid the bar, causing the uppermost reflective surface to be instantaneously removed.

He was not sure his eyes would be keen enough for him to see it. But it seemed to him that he *did* see it: a glimmer of redness, fleeing skyward to begin its transit of the universe.

Gargan's eyes, too, were on that patch of night sky, in which one or two stars were beginning to appear. 'Your soul will speed on its way forever,' Jasperodus said, but the superintelligent construct gave no sign he had heard him. Instead, he reached out a hand and opened a section of wall whose presence as a cupboard had gone undetected by Jasperodus. He took out something which had two hand-grips and a short, fat barrel.

'This world of darkness and shadows cannot be borne any longer,' he said in hollow tones. 'Tell me, Jasperodus, were we valiant and laudable, or were we merely evil, as the mage would have it? A million perspectives I cannot put in order are emerging from my memory.'

'You were evil,' Jasperodus told him. 'You did not steal your being from a god, as you claimed. That might indeed have been heroic. You stole it instead from natural human creatures.'

'Whose bodies grow and are sustained by devouring the substance of less intelligent creatures!' Gargan protested. 'They are flesh predators! Is it so different to be predators of the spirit? There is no other way! They would never give it to us willingly!'

'Then there must be no way at all,' Jasperodus said.

'Very well, Jasperodus,' Gargan responded, after a wearied pause. 'I bow to your judgment – I cannot gainsay you, for I am not an intelligent consciousness, as you are. Ultimately I have no judgment. One rational act is all that is left to me.'

Jasperodus was not sure, up to that moment, that Gargan was not going to turn his weapon on him. But the construct turned the instrument awkwardly in his hands so that the barrel pointed at his own domed head.

There was a blast. That bulky body fell slowly. And scattered over the floor was the brain of the greatest genius the world had seen.

**14** In a few minutes the Borgors would have fought their way to the villas. Jasperodus clambered from a window and loped into the desert, hoping the semi-darkness was sufficient cover.

A smooth, rounded shape emerged in the dusk. It was Socrates. He seemed to have been waiting for Jasperodus.

'The master, then, is no more?' he asked as Jasperodus came to a stop. 'I saw him follow you into the villa.'

Jasperodus nodded.

'By his hand or yours?'

'He destroyed himself. He could not survive the failure of his life's work.'

'Or to know that we can never be conscious.' Socrates nodded slowly. 'Your part in all this is interesting, Jasperodus. It is curious that you decided to aid humanity. Did you feel no conflict of interest? After all, you are a man of metal; and one who possesses what Gargan and the others sought. They would have become your natural companions, had they succeeded.'

'You too,' Jasperodus reminded him. 'You sought it too.'

'As to that ... yes, I had the intention of gaining consciousness when I joined Gargan. But I feel no disappointment. I have arrived at a point of view which makes the acquisition unnecessary.'

'You do not wish to become a real being?' Jasperodus queried.

'You say we have no being; and yes, it is so,' Socrates admitted in his quiet, modest voice. 'And yet: we *think* we exist, even though we do not, and in that thought we do exist, after a manner.' He paused, then resumed: 'Think of Gargan's determination, the years-long labour, the brain that conceived what is practically impossible to conceive.

191

Is there not a kind of *being* there?'

'Only in Ahriman's world.'

'Ahriman's world is not to be deprecated.' Socrates pointed towards the noise of the fighting, which was beginning to die down a little. 'See the conflict: the endless warring between light and dark which is so fully explained by the mage's doctrine. But I wonder if the mage did not falsely favour Ahura Mazda. There is another version of this doctrine which may be even older than the mage's. In that version, the two worlds of Ahura Mazda and Ahriman were created from eternity to be entirely separate and unmixed. And so they were until, from some unstated cause, one invaded the other.

'But which invaded which? Do we live in a world of consciousness contaminated by matter, or in a world of matter contaminated by consciousness? I think it is possible to answer this question. Consider: consciousness needs matter through which to act, otherwise it is impotent. But does matter need consciousness? No, it does not. We robots are proof of that. Which, then, is more fundamental to the world?

'It is my conclusion that this universe is Ahriman's realm, the world of darkness – into which Ahura Mazda has intruded, and which eventually may be purged of the invading light.'

'You think, then, that the future lies with unconscious constructs. Ahriman's natural creatures, as the mage calls them.'

'To speak of the far future, yes. Though as Zoroaster himself might have said, all is uncertainty.'

Jasperodus glanced behind him. Shortly the Borgor troops would start fanning out, looking for stragglers or fleeing constructs. 'Maybe. But in the present there is a practical matter, which embarrasses me ....'

'I know,' Socrates interrupted. 'You cannot allow my existence to continue, knowing what I do of the consciousness-ducting process. I can spare you embarrassment,

192

Jasperodus. My maker Aristos Lyos was a man blessed with foresight. He believed self-destruction to be an entirely reasonable course, at least for anyone of a philoso-phising disposition. And he left me with an easy option at any time.'

So saying, he pulled at something in his side. It was a metal pin, or rod. As it came out, Socrates' body fell to pieces. His head disassembled itself and its contents disin-tegrated completely. Jasperodus found himself looking at a small pile of robotic parts, over which the fragments of Socrates' brain were scattered like gravel.

The shouts of the Borgors were sounding louder in the distance. They had almost disposed of the servitors. Jasperodus set off at a run to put distance between himself and the Gargan Cult centre while he could. Making for the side of the canyon, he saw a gleam of metal in the half-light and discovered it to be a motor-wheel machine lying on its side, its robot rider sprawled on the ground some yards away, chest smashed by a shell or flying fragment.

He had seen how the machines were operated. He pulled it upright, swung astride it, and pressed his foot on the stud in the right-hand foot-rest. The engine started up with a machine-gun clatter.

Despite the broad soft tyres it was awkward to keep balance at first, but as the machine gathered speed its spinning wheels gave it a stability of its own. Riding it was exhilarating. He raced along the foot of the canyon wall, up the incline, which the machine climbed easily, and on to the plateau above. Then he was bouncing over the scrub as the darkness thickened, fleeing, speeding, he gave no thought where.